D0779880

Also available in the
TOM CLANCY'S NET FORCE EXPLORERS series

Tom Clancy's
Net Force Explorers:
The Great Race

Created by Tom Clancy and Steve Pieczenik

HEADLINE
FEATURE

First published in 1999
by HEADLINE BOOK PUBLISHING

A HEADLINE FEATURE paperback

10 9 8 7 6 5 4 3 2 1

ISBN 0 7472 6165 2

Typeset by
Letterpart Limited, Reigate, Surrey

Printed and bound in Great Britain by
Mackays of Chatham plc, Chatham, Kent

HEADLINE BOOK PUBLISHING
A division of the Hodder Headline Group
338 Euston Road
London NW1 3BH
www.headline.co.uk
www.hodderheadline.com

Acknowledgements

We'd like to thank the following people, without whom this book would have not been possible: Bill McCay, for help in rounding out the mauscript; Martin H. Greenberg, Larry Segriff, Denise Little, and John Helfers at Tekno Books; Mitchell Rubenstein and Laurie Silvers at BIG Entertainment; Tom Colgan of Penguin Putnam Inc; Robert Youdelman, Esquire; and Tom Mallon, Esquire; and Robert Gottlieb of the William Morris Agency, agent and friend. We much appreciated the help.

Chapter One

Without taking his eyes from the readouts on the console in front of him, Leif Anderson pursed his lips and blew. He was hoping the gust of breath would deflect the bead of sweat heading down toward the tip of his nose.

His attempt failed.

Leif tried a quick head shake. That only made it worse. The drip took off, floating in microgravity until it hit the face shield of Leif's helmet. There it splashed like a raindrop – except this was on the inside of the clear plastic panel. A set of numbers on the screen, blocked by the droplet, turned into an unreadable blur.

Leif's breath hissed through his teeth. He *needed* those readouts if he was supposed to regulate the braking on this bucket. And there was no other way they were landing on Mars.

He glanced at his fellow Net Force Explorers – not that there was much to see, with them all swathed in space suits. David Gray sat at the Mars lander's piloting position. Leif knew that his friend's face would be as set and hard as if it were carved from ebony. He was the one who'd ordered the crew to button up their space suits. After all, the trickiest part of the whole trip was coming up.

1

Matt Hunter was like a bird dog on point before his copilot's console. Leif could imagine his friend's eager brown eyes taking in every bit of data. Andy Moore sat in front of his controls with an almost disinterested slouch – but what could you expect from the joker of the group?

As for Leif, he was 'enjoying' all the smells a person could possibly enjoy while being locked up in a plastic and metal cocoon and sweating like a pig. It was bad enough breathing recycled air and living in cramped quarters with three other guys. But when you were stuck in cramped quarters with *yourself* . . .

The trip to Mars was no easy job. Just getting off the ground had been a considerable effort. The Mars spacecraft alone weighed in at 2500 metric tons – more than five and a half *million* pounds. And that didn't count all the additional tons of docking hardware to get the bucket into orbit, nor the fuel, nor the little details like food and air for the crew of four for a round trip that would take a good three years.

Adding to the difficulties of the trip were the inevitable changes that accumulated in the human body after months without gravity. Leif didn't like the weird posture his body took on when the muscles designed to hold him upright against Earth's pull had nothing to work against. It took a regimen of relentless exercise throughout the trip to keep a person's body from turning into a cloud of boneless mush.

Proceeding from orbit around Earth, they'd reached Mars and swung into a circle around that planet. That had been hairy enough – the Mars Observer craft had been lost back in 1993 during orbital insertion.

But that was the equipment of twenty years ago. And the Mars Observer had been an unmanned craft, operated by remote control from the Earth. On a job where every split second counted, it took radio waves an average of four and a half minutes to reach the space probe – space is big, even when something's moving at the speed of light.

Their old bucket didn't have light-speed engines, just good old-fashioned rockets. But it also had a four-man crew aboard to ride down in the Mars lander, explore, then launch up the Earth return craft – two hundred metric tons altogether. All they had to do was balance it on top of a jet of white-hot gases until they touched down on the Martian surface with a bump – and not a crash.

Leif initiated another braking sequence – the last before touchdown – and prepared to become just another passenger. David and Matt would have the job of goosing the bucket upright during its descent with attitude rockets.

The effect of the retrorockets hit, giving Leif and his fellow Net Force Explorers the brief sensation of weight.

Then they were weightless again – and red lights lit up all over Leif's board. He punched the buttons and flipped switches, his fingers clumsy in their gauntlets.

'Something's wrong with the fuel pumps – they cut out in the middle of the sequence!' he reported into his helmet mike.

This was the worst of bad news. They were dropping swiftly through the thin Martian atmosphere. Even though the planet below was pulling at them with much less than Earth's gravity, they were moving at a terrifying clip.

And the brakes didn't seem to be working.

Leif kept trying to troubleshoot the fuel-delivery system, wishing he could crack open the faceplate on the helmet and wipe his dripping face. The inside of his suit seemed very hot and damp right now. 'I can't find what's wrong!' he said, trying to keep the panic out of his voice.

'I'm going to try to trigger the retros manually – prepare for a jolt,' David warned.

The engines roared, then spluttered, roared, and spluttered again. The vibrations shuddered through the metallic structure of the ship, carrying the news of impending disaster with them.

That was *not* what Leif wanted to hear. He turned to the readouts, trying to catch an indication of their speed.

Too high. *Way* too high.

'Do we just abort the mission?' Matt broke in on the circuit. 'Light up the engine on the return craft and get out of here?'

'I – I don't think we can do that,' David's voice was numb as he tried to deal with a situation he'd never counted on.

Seconds ticked away as the Net Force Explorers tried more and more desperate measures either to stop their fall or to head back to space again.

Leif imagined the view below them. Mars had already dominated the vista through the observation ports for weeks, a ruddy pockmarked ball that had grown larger and larger. It has almost been as if Leif could reach through the heavy plastic and grab the planet in the palm of his hand.

Of course, trying that would let the vacuum of space into the cramped crew quarters, removing the atmosphere, sucking the very breath of life out of their lungs, leaving four asphyxiated, freeze-dried corpses floating in a derelict ship. The airlessness outside, or rather, near-airlessness – they were already in the tenuous wisp that Mars called an atmosphere – meant that they could see every feature of the planet's surface with uncanny clarity.

It was also the reason why David had insisted on full

space suits and closed helmets. He wanted to protect the crew members in case of a bumpy landing. David just hadn't planned on taking the situation to such an extreme.

They wouldn't bump when they hit the surface.

The landing would fall somewhere between a *splat!* and a *kaboom!*

Leif gritted his teeth. This was not the time to think about how anything would *fall*.

David continued the struggle all the way down. Leif could imagine the rust-red, stony landscape coming closer and closer—

'I've had enough of this!' Andy Moore suddenly burst out. 'I'm sweating like a pig!' He opened the plate in his helmet and wiped a face so pale, faint freckles stood out.

David half-twisted in his acceleration couch. 'What are you doing?'

'It won't matter in another second,' Andy flared. 'This is nothing a suit could help me through!'

David shouted, in rage, or fear, or perhaps a combination of both.

Leif arranged himself on his acceleration couch. It *was* warm in the control room. Was the Martian atmosphere going to ignite them like an oversized falling star?

He took a deep breath . . .

And the crash came.

Chapter Two

'Huuuuuuuuuuuuggggh!' Leif nearly fell out of his computer-link chair when the system crashed. He slouched against the luxurious, contour-hugging foam material, rubbing his temples. Then he got up, wobbling slightly, and took a few steps.

The computer-link chair reminded him too much of the acceleration couch aboard the ill-fated Mars lander.

Could have been worse, he told himself. *If we'd been on the real thing, instead of just a virtual-reality simulation of it, we'd be a messy spot on the Mars landscape.*

Leif paced around his room, his hands rubbing at his temples and the back of his neck, trying to massage away the headache – or rather, the pain around the circuitry implanted under his red hair. Those implants allowed him to interface with the computer-link chair and enter the Net, the global web-work where computers talked to one another, transferring money, information – and any kind of fantasy that the wildest imaginations could come up with.

Through the magic of veeyar – VR, or virtual reality – Leif had been many places and done many things. A couple of times a week he was a wizard on a pseudo-medieval gameworld. His Net Force adventures in that world had turned out better than his stint as a crewman on

David Gray's Mars expedition.

David's private space program was a hobby, rather than a commercial venture like the lands of Sarxos, the gameworld where Leif practiced wizardry. David enjoyed engineering virtual copies of space hardware – usually the great unmanned probes of the early days of space exploration. His Net programs were some of the best, even though they could leave a person with a wicked headache after an unplanned bounce out of a scenario. David believed that even virtual mistakes should have consequences.

Leif doubted that David had planned to make the consequences this severe. Leif was currently extra-sensitive to any kind of implant problem. He'd recently suffered serious implant trauma when a would-be prankster had circumvented veeyar safety protocols to add a real kick to the virtual bullets he was firing. Now it didn't take much to give him a killer headache. Not that Leif complained to the guys about his problem. And he figured it was worth taking the risk in exchange for the privilege of going along on the journey.

The Mars expedition had been David's most ambitious effort to date, requiring a four-person crew and multiple sessions in veeyar over several weeks – David only simulated the critical moments in the months-long flight, rather than the whole space voyage. The technology was antique, dating back to 2010, fifteen years ago. With today's nuclear-electric space drive, a voyage to Mars took only a couple of months.

Leif's father was particularly proud of doing his bit in space. He'd ordered his company to help fund the basic research for the new drive.

And made a handsome profit on it, Leif thought with a grin. *I guess the family spirits punished me for traveling the old-fashioned way – even in simulation.*

He sighed. At least the worst of his computer-crash-inspired headache had faded. Leif accessed his computer – by voice, this time – and asked for a hologram link to David's system.

A moment later, a three-dimensional image of David's face swam into existence over the computer console. The seventeen-year-old looked no better than Leif felt, despite the burnished ebony skin that hid any post-crash pallor. Maybe David even looked little worse – after all, it was David's brainchild that had crashed. Still, he summoned up a smile when he saw his caller.

'Hey, Leif.'

'Sorry, David.'

David shrugged. 'My own fault, I expect,' he said. 'I make the hardware too real. The Mars astronauts had years to familiarize themselves with the equipment. All we had was a quick-immersion course.'

'We got pretty close,' Leif tried to comfort his friend.

'A little *too* close, while moving at several miles per second,' David retorted. 'You know what they say – it's not the fall that kills you, it's the sudden stop.'

'How are Matt and Andy?' Leif asked about his other crewmen/friends.

'They both buzzed in before you – they're fine. In fact, they're stopping by to watch this week's *Ultimate Frontier* with me.' David hesitated. 'If you wanted to plug in—'

'Thanks, but I don't think so.' David and his friends all lived in the Washington, D.C., area. Leif was at his parents' apartment in New York City. He didn't mind making a quick virtual visit to David's house, but linking into the Net for a long period of time right now would just intensify his headache.

'Then I guess we'll see you at the next Net Force Explorers meeting,' David said.

Leif nodded, wincing a little – implant headaches were miserable things. 'Later. Take it easy.'

'You too.'

They cut their link.

Stepping over to the bed, Leif plopped down and caught his reflection in the mirror. He was slender, and his landing was graceful enough – a genetic favor from his mother, a former ballerina. His red hair was a bit tousled from his attempts to make that blasted headache go away. Leif supposed he was good-looking, in a sharp-featured kind of way. Just the thing for a future globe-trotting playboy.

Right now, though, his blue eyes were soft and there was a silly, fond smile on his lips. The Net Force Explorers had offered him a welcome escape from the world of the rich and jaded . . . one that didn't involve bizarre fantasies.

Net Force was a government agency, a subdivision of the FBI tasked with the job of policing the Net. Net Force agents found themselves up against terrorists, criminals, foreign governments up to no good, and even thrill-seeking kids out for a virtual spree.

The Net Force Explorers weren't exactly Net Force's junior auxiliary. They got some physical training, provided by Net Force's Marine component, but the Net Force Explorers spent more time learning about the Net than about being cops.

What Leif especially liked was the comradeship with his fellow Net Force Explorers. Even though he saw them more often in veeyar than in the flesh, these guys kept him grounded in reality.

Take David Gray – where else but Net Force Explorers would a rich kid in a New York penthouse end up hanging out with a young black guy whose father was a D.C. cop?

The truth was, between Net Force and the Net Force Explorers, Leif had wound up in some pretty interesting situations – even if he sometimes ended up in a crash.

Still smiling, Leif got up, headed for the kitchen, and made himself a snack. Food usually helped these head-aches go away. When he finished, he looked at his watch. Hey, *Ultimate Frontier* would be on in a few minutes!

Leif padded over to the living room and warmed up the holo-suite. As usual, Dad had paid for the very best. The effect of the three-D projection was just a little short of actual veeyar.

The theme music came on, and Leif seemed to swoop through space, veering around stars and planets.

Maybe this is what the old Mars bucket needed, he thought. *Computer-controlled everything and sound effects to let us swooosssh! through airless space without too much interference from the laws of physic*s.

The seemingly never-ending saga of the star cruiser *Constellation* was a spin-off from an earlier series, which in turn had been spawned by a decades-older version, and so on and so on, back to the days of flatscreen television.

Leif settled back on the couch. *Okay*, he thought, *let's see what Captain Venn and the crew get up to this time around . . .*

In Washington, D.C., David Gray and his friends sat in a crowded living room, watching *Ultimate Frontier*. They were all on the couch. David's mom had the armchair, and David's kid brothers James and Tommy lay on the floor, staring up at the holo image.

Andy Moore was in what David called their friend's 'motormouth mode.' With a big grin on his freckled face,

Andy kept up a steady stream of talk, goofing on the plot and the characters.

In this episode, the *Constellation* had the unwelcome job of convoying representatives from several alien races to a major diplomatic conference. Of course somebody was trying to assassinate the various representatives.

Mrs Gray sighed as the Nimboid ambassador, an energy-being composed of ever-twining glowing tendrils, was somehow discharged into the ship's electrical systems.

'No big deal,' Andy hooted. 'The engineer will somehow figure a way to shunt the ambassador into the computers.'

'This isn't a rerun, is it?' Matt Hunter asked with a skeptical glance at his pal.

'No, but that doesn't stop the writers from rerunning the same old ideas. Good old Mr Pendennis – did you ever notice almost all chief engineers in this universe are Celtic? Frankly, I think they're pushing the envelope with a Cornishman. But anyway, Mr Pendennis will whomp up the magic thingamajig that will save the alien's life.'

'I just think the aliens are too weird-looking nowadays,' Mrs Gray complained. 'In the old days, on the flatscreen—'

'Oh, come on, Mrs G!' Andy burst out. Then he looked embarrassed. 'Sorry. But the makeup budgets must have come from studio candy sales back then. Either that, or all those aliens lived on planets with very bright suns. They got big wrinkles on their foreheads or between their eyes from squinting in the sunlight.' He tried to scrunch up his nose and forehead to demonstrate his point.

David laughed. 'Nowadays, the aliens are all based on demographics – audiences the show wants to appeal to.'

'What do you mean?' Matt asked.

'The producers of this show want it to air all over the

world,' David explained. 'Since the U.S. is the primary market, the Galactic federation is sort of a funhouse mirror reflection of our government and culture, projected into the future. But look at some of the alien races. The Laragants – taller than we are, beautiful like statues—'

'Stretched, idealized humans,' Andy broke in.

'With lots of wisdom, and taste up the wazoo,' David finished. '*Constellation* crew members who encounter them often come off looking . . . well, boorish.' He glanced at his friends. 'They're tailor-made to fit in with European self-perceptions.'

'Hunh!' Matt said. 'I guess I never really looked at it before. The Arcturan Co-Prosperity Sphere – that's kind of self-explanatory.'

David nodded. 'Their culture is supposed to attract Asians in general, and Japanese in particular. While the Setangis – breakaway colony worlds exploited by the former Laragant Empire – are supposed to appeal to the emergent African states.'

'That all makes a sort of twisted sense,' Andy admitted. 'But what about the Thuriens? Those guys are treacherous, warmongering slimeballs—'

'They're xenophobic, totally without conscience in dealing with other races,' David corrected. 'Their culture doesn't believe in individuality – yet worships personal bravery.'

'They're the all-purpose villains on the series,' Matt said.

'Yet they sometimes seem almost heroic.' David nodded toward the holo-image, where a Thurien guard, protecting his ambassador, took on four *Constellation* crewmen. The silver-skinned humanoid, his high-cheekboned face absolutely featureless, went into a wild, rolling attack, dropping three of the red-shirted security officers before he himself was shot.

'I just thought that no-face thing was a cheap trick – to save on actors and make up for the expensive hologram characters that appear in some episodes. All those weird differences came in from the different writers.' Matt shrugged. 'You know, if things get boring, throw in the Thuriens.'

'I still don't know anybody on Earth who's like them,' Andy challenged.

'Then you should talk to Captain Winters,' David replied, mentioning the name of the former Marine officer who served as the Net Force Explorers' liaison to Net Force. 'He actually fought them a few years ago.'

'You mean when he was part of the peacekeeping force in the Balkans?' Andy said in disbelief.

Matt just stared. 'The Carpathian Alliance!'

An area with three religions, four languages, two alphabets, and too many national and ethnic groups, the Balkans had been a world trouble spot throughout the last thirty years, and on an occasional basis for centuries. The last time fighting had broken out, the enemies of peace in that region had formed an uneasy alliance, combining a set of '-isms' that most people thought had disappeared with the end of the twentieth century.

The Carpathian Alliance brought together believers in fascism and communism – doctrines that in other times and places had fought wars against one another. Into this ugly brew they had mixed a horrible strand of racism – and under these discredited banners, the Alliance had invaded their 'inferior' neighbors.

Their armies had been beaten back, but the Carpathian Alliance's fighters had been more like gangs of criminals than soldiers. Even after they'd been beaten, they'd continued a 'war' of terrorism and assassination. The lands they'd attacked had gathered together into Slobodan Narodny, the Free State. Yet the Carpathian Alliance managed to survive, a loose collection of dictatorships clinging to power in the rugged Balkan Mountains – just waiting for another chance to make trouble.

Andy shook his head in disbelief. 'Why would anybody bother sucking up to – what? A couple of million wackos?'

'More like ten million additional viewers,' David corrected. 'Besides, what does it hurt to present them as courageous enemies?'

'It hurts every American boy and girl who died fighting them,' Mrs Gray suddenly said. She glanced at David. 'I wish you hadn't told me about this. Somehow, I don't think I'll ever enjoy this show again.'

They watched the rest of the episode in embarrassed silence. Sure enough, Mr Pendennis managed to shift the Nimboid ambassador out of the electrical system, into the computers, and finally reconstituted him. The Thuriens turned out not to be behind the assassinations. The culprit was a disaffected 'artificial person' servant of the Laragants.

Commander Dominic, Captain Venn's piratically handsome second in command, managed to subdue the android assassin in a flurry of microgravity martial-arts moves.

'Stuntman,' Andy muttered. 'He lands there without even mussing his hair.'

The Thurien ambassador, He-Who-Leads-In-Conflict-Without-War, saluted Commander Dominic, then turned to Captain Venn. 'Your people did well to avert catastrophe. Perhaps we should attempt more non-warlike conflicts.'

'Contests,' Captain Venn diplomatically amended.

The Thurien leader nodded. 'Each of the starfaring races represented here has a facility for the training of young astrogators—'

'The Academy,' Dominic said.

'Perhaps a race,' the Thurien suggested. 'To teach the coming generation the ways of non-conflict.'

The credits began to float past a planetary disk when they suddenly shifted to one side. Commander Dominic appeared – or rather Lance Snowdon, the actor who portrayed him.

Snowdon had abandoned his Fleet tunic for a rather loud turtleneck sweater. He grinned as the theme music receded. 'Just a brief word from real life to all *Ultimate Frontier* fans under eighteen years of age,' he said. 'Pinnacle Productions is running a competition for all the young designers in our audience. Create a virtual racing yacht for any of the civilizations in this evening's episode, and win a chance to participate with a four-person crew in a show about the race of the twenty-sixth century!

'Technical specs are available at the Pinnacle Productions Net site, subreference Great Race.'

The actor went on with a rap about dates and eligibility, but David didn't hear that. He was looking from Andy to Matt, who were staring at him expectantly.

'So?' Andy asked. 'Are we going to enter?'

David shook his head. 'Pretty ambitious, don't you think,' he said, 'for a team whose last project just crashed and died?'

Chapter Three

David was still laughing off the idea of joining the Ultimate Frontier competition when a muted chime filled the room. His brother Tommy hopped up from the floor. 'Somebody's calling!' he announced.

Tommy raced off to the hall and returned a moment later. 'It's your friend Leif,' he told David.

David stepped round to the secondary holo display that served as the family's communication center. As soon as he came into view, Leif said, 'I wanted to make sure I had a place on the crew of your racing yacht.'

'What racing yacht?' David replied. 'Matt and Andy were just talking the same dopiness—'

'Hey, we went on a ride to Mars with you. We even got killed with you.' Leif gave him a grin. 'It's the least you could do.'

David felt a little embarrassed at the belief the guys had in him. 'I suppose I could take a look at the technical guidelines on their Net site.'

'Excellent!' Leif's grin grew broader. 'Hollywood, here we come!'

'Hollywood?' David echoed.

Leif gave him a sharp look. 'Weren't you listening? The winners actually go to Hollywood and appear in the racing episode. We meet the stars of the series' – his grin became wicked – 'and all the "Ultimate" alien babes who turn up in each episode.'

David laughed. 'Don't get your hopes up. The alien babes are usually reserved for Commander Dominic. And there's still the problem of beating out everybody else who'll be designing a ship for the Galactic Federation. Frontie Net sites have probably been discussing this contest for months.' David had used the slang term for fans of *Ultimate Frontier*.

'Fronties?' Leif snorted. 'I'm not worried about those get-a-lifes. Just get started on a good design.' He hesitated for a second. 'And if you need anything—'

David waved away the delicate offer of financial help. 'Thanks. I'll get on the Net as soon as Matt and Andy head home.'

'Just tell them to get out of there and stop distracting you from important work,' Leif commanded.

David laughed and cut the connection. Then he headed back to the living room to make his announcement. The Net Force Explorers weren't heading for Mars anymore. Instead, they'd reach for the stars.

The four boys floated in space – cyberspace, this time, visiting David in veeyar. Before them floated the wireframe image of their starship – David's first draft, as he'd warned them.

Its main hull was a simplified arrow shape, twice as long as it was wide, four planes converging to a needle point. A pair of stubby wings angled down from the top decks, terminating in the familiar dumbbell shapes of the engine pods. A third wing rose up like a dorsal fin from the rear of the arrowhead, carrying another engine. The base of the third wing spread out – housing the ship's bridge.

'Nice look,' Matt commented. 'Federation ships always go for clean lines.'

'It's more streamlined than I'd have expected,' Leif said.

'Guilty,' David admitted. 'In the vacuum of space, the profile of the ship doesn't really matter, unless you also have to operate in planetary atmospheres,' David explained. 'The race scenario doesn't call for that, so we can ditch the mass required for insulation and landing gear and so on. It makes us that much faster and more maneuverable.'

'But that tri-wing structure – nobody's used that arrangement since the last flatscreen series, back around the turn of the century,' Andy objected. He gave the others a supercilious stare, holding up a virtual icon that looked like a datascrip. 'Hey, I did my research. Right here, I've got every ship design that ever appeared in all the various series, going back to the beginning.' He grinned. 'Even ships that only appeared in the background during planet shots.'

Andy tossed the icon out into space and gave an order. 'Computer, find the closest referents to the existing design from this collection.'

A quiet voice like a whisper of breeze replied, 'Processing.'

In a moment, two similar shapes floated alongside David's design. These were finished renditions, their skins the familiar silver-blue of the Federation fleet.

'A long-range scout and a priority courier craft.' Leif's voice was impressed as he read the specifications that floated beside each. 'Did you base your design on these?'

David shook his head. 'When would I have time to do that research, between school and people calling down from New York asking how things were coming along? I developed the basic design through computer analysis of the show's technical specs. This layout of the propulsion systems and this superstructure for the ship came up as the best if you're looking for speed and maneuverability.'

He gave the others a hard look. 'It's not a case of figuring how to tie a ship onto an engine. It's a case of making sure the engines can do what they're supposed to without ripping the ship apart. The structure has to be strong enough to handle the repeated stresses of acceleration and deceleration as well as sudden changes in course, and the propulsion systems have to be carefully calibrated. I ran some tests and that's what I came up with.'

Pointing to the wireframe figure, he said, 'That's the best configuration for a small-crew, maneuverable ship. The shape makes for cramped quarters, but houses the necessary life-support and hull-stabilization systems. The small size cuts down on mass, so we're faster. But I'm not cutting corners on life support or hull stabilizers.' He grinned. 'Otherwise, we don't live to win.'

He pointed to the flared housing for the dorsal engine. 'There are places I've sacrificed mass for speed. For example, if we really max out all three of our engines for too long, the stresses might tear the ship apart. On the other hand, I like the built-in redundancy of extra engines – that was how the series started out, before the spacecraft began looking more like flying cities – or garbage dumps.'

David glanced at Andy. 'Thanks for digging these up. They'll be a help in determining where the machinery goes aboard the *Onrust*.'

'*Onrust*?' Matt echoed. 'That doesn't sound like Federation English.' He shot a puzzled look toward Leif. 'Sounds German, or Swedish—'

'It's Dutch,' David said. 'Translates as restless. But it's also the name of an interesting exploration ship. Adrian Block built the *Onrust* while he was wintering on Manhattan Island a few centuries ago. He and his crew used the skiff to explore Long Island Sound – a voyage of more than a hundred miles – to link up with the only other Dutch oceangoing vessel in the area. You see, Block's original ship, the *Tiger*, burnt and sank. If he and his men didn't catch up with that other boat, they'd have lost their only ride home.'

'Sort of like us with the Mars lander,' Andy said, suddenly catching on. 'We crashed and burned. But by building this baby, we'll make up for that, right?'

'I hope so,' Matt said. 'You and David know more about this stuff than I do. If you needed to simulate a car or a plane, though . . .'

'Don't distract our engineering geniuses,' Leif warned. 'We want this thing to be ready before Pinnacle Productions' cutoff date.'

'We'll be ready,' David assured him. 'From here on, it's just a case of calibration.' He laughed. 'I'll tell you one thing – this make-believe technology is a lot easier to handle than the real stuff we were trying. According to the *Ultimate Frontier* specs, computers will project courses, balance systems, even interface between humans and the controls. I've already gone through the technical immersion the production company provided.'

He rolled his eyes. 'It's a *lot* easier than what we went through for the Mars voyage.'

'Something on your mind, son?' Magnus Anderson asked a week or so later, looking across the breakfast table. 'You look about a million miles away.'

'Make that a few light-years,' Leif admitted, glancing from his father to his mother. Natalya Anderson looked slim and elegant, eating some sort of yogurt-and-barley concoction. Magnus, on the other hand, liked to have what he called 'real food' in the morning – in this case, eggs and bacon. Leif, not much of a breakfast eater, just had an English muffin.

'I just went through the technical immersion for my crew position in the Great Race,' Leif explained.

'That's right,' his father said. 'The first heats, or tryouts, whatever you call them, must be coming up soon.'

Leif nodded. 'And we're all ready to go – at least I'll be, as soon as all the new stuff crammed into my skull settles in.'

'You're sure?' his mother said worriedly.

Magnus Anderson shook his head. 'Natalya, deep immersion is *not* brainwashing, whatever your dancer friends think. It's more like sleep-learning.'

'We learned every step while we were wide awake,' the former ballerina said, repeating something Leif and his father heard every time they took the learning shortcut of immersion. 'And we practiced them until they were a part of us, right down in the muscle memory.'

'Oh, we'll be practicing on our ship, too,' Leif quickly said. 'What I got last night was a good theoretical knowledge of how a starship works – at least how one works on *Ultimate Frontier*.'

He grinned. 'I still have to find out how that shapes up with the practical experience of driving our little racer.'

His father shook his head again. 'This virtuality business has gone in directions I couldn't even have imagined when the technology first came out.' He hesitated for a second. 'If you and your friends need any technical assistance, just call my office.'

'Thanks, Dad.' Leif was touched by his father's offer.

His mother just laughed. 'Of course,' she said. 'And remember, Andersons are expected to come in first.'

The crew members of the *Onrust* cut their veeyar links in grim silence at the end of the race. Leif immediately accessed the system at Anderson Investment Multinational and arranged a conference call. Seconds later, holo-images of David, Matt, and Andy glared out of the air over his parents' console.

'Second!' Andy burst out, fuming. 'We could have been first, if you hadn't let that guy muscle his way in front of us.'

'That guy brought a whole new meaning to the phrase "a crash course in piloting," ' Matt said sourly. 'He was willing to risk a collision that would have taken us both out of the competition.'

'We could have jockeyed around them if we had to.' David's face was calm, his eyes glancing at something off to the side. 'The official standings were just posted. Our times still give us a place in the quarterfinals.'

'As a wild card,' Andy sulked.

'More like a dark horse,' Leif suggested. 'The other racers still don't know every trick we've got up our sleeves. But we've learned a lot. For instance, those bozos who cut us off – that wasn't a kamikaze stunt. It was bad ship handling. I was checking the readings from their engines The engineer lost control of the drives – he was supposed to boot both of them, but only one cut in, making them swerve. We now know to stay away from them.'

'Let 'em crash into somebody else next time,' Andy quickly agreed.

'We'll just stay ahead of them – and anyone else.' David's voice was quiet, but there was a trace of steel in it.

Leif grinned. *You don't fool me with that cool act.* He thought. *Coming in second has you as riled as Andy.* He shrugged philosophically. If it had to happen, this was the best time – when it didn't count all that much.

But there were still three elimination rounds to get through. From this point on, it had to be number one all the way . . .

'We're still ahead of them – don't blow it now!' Matt said from his position as scanning officer.

The main viewscreen was split to show the course ahead and the other racers behind them. But Leif wasn't about to shift his attention to see how they were doing. He had his hands – and his brains – full, monitoring the bridge's engineering station.

It was easier than trying to land on Mars. The computers did a lot of the work, like maintaining the artificial gravity. But so much of the race environment was chaotic and unpredictable, it still required a human touch to balance the acceleration of three engines, keep the ship's structure stable, and make the split-second course adjustments for maximum speed. David had sliced the soy protein mighty fine with his final design. They were flying a gnat of a ship with engines meant to propel a patrol frigate with a crew of fifty.

The bridge of the *Onrust* was considerably more spacious than the Mars lander, although it would have fit in the mythical captain's bathroom that they never saw aboard the *Constellation*.

Matt and Andy sat at adjoining consoles facing the

23

viewscreen. David's command chair nearly touched Leif's engineering terminal.

At least they didn't have to wear space suits to operate this sucker.

'Leif!' Andy called. 'We're coming up on the last course marker. It all depends on how fast we can make this final turn. Can you give me any more power?'

Leif looked worriedly at his displays. 'Hull stabilization is maxed out. I can't—'

'The traditional response is, "It's gonna blow," ' Andy interrupted.

'Try diverting the power from life support,' David said.

'We'll be running in the red – the danger zone,' Leif warned.

David examined the view ahead. 'There's a planet just beyond the marker. Suppose we used their gravity well for a slingshot effect?'

Andy recalculated his course. 'It can be done, but we'll end up grazing the planet's atmosphere.'

David leaned back in his seat – but Leif saw his fingers were clenched on the arms. 'We can do that.'

I hope we can, Leif thought.

The space-buoy marking the course for this elimination round came up with frightening speed. Then they were past and going into their wild turn. The maneuver was more than the artificial gravity could compensate for. Everyone clung to their stations as they were jostled by a force that made the deck seem to heel over at a dangerous angle.

In the viewscreen, the planet swelled like a big, hungry face.

Leif tore his eyes away to keep checking his readouts. Hull temperature – rising fast. Stabilizing shields – threatening failure. If they gave out, the ship would be torn to bits in the planet's upper atmosphere.

We'll make a heck of a meteor shower, he thought. *I wonder if this place is supposed to be inhabited.* If so, the crew of the *Onrust* might expect a reprimand for pulling this stunt.

He kept his thoughts to himself, merely reporting the growing forces on the ship's hull.

And then, miraculously, they were past, in open space, the dangerous stresses fading away.

Leif let out a breath he hadn't realized he'd been holding.

'Hey, David?' he said. 'Is it me, or is it getting stuffy in here?'

'Re-energize life support,' David said, his attention fully on the viewscreen, which showed their pursuers – the other racers – coming up on the buoy. 'If they can cut the turn finer than we did,' he muttered, 'we've lost.'

The leader of the pack had the brutal lines of a Thurien sword-ship rather than those of a Federation Fleet vessel.

Call it a knife-ship, Leif corrected himself. Most of its length was 'handle' – a single, grossly overpowered hyper-engine that gave them terrifying speed on the straightaways. Fortunately, it didn't take turns easily.

The sword-ship's captain now gambled on a tricky end-for-end turn as he flashed past the course marker.

It would have won him the race – if his engine hadn't blown.

The viewscreen suddenly darkened, protecting the eyes of the *Onrust*'s crew from the sudden flare of energy. What had been a ship was now a cloud of white-hot plasma, a miniature sun spreading across the courses of the other racers. They scrambled to avoid the unexpected obstacle.

Leif switched his attention to the rearview screen. The

marker buoy was behind them now, going up in a smaller flash as the plasma cloud engulfed it. Several ships weren't going to be able to avoid the cloud altogether –

More flashes appeared as other racers suffered catastrophic failures. Those who managed to avoid the disaster couldn't make their turns after their emergency course diversions.

By the time the remaining competitors reorganized themselves, the *Onrust* was halfway through the final straightaway to the finish line.

David surprised Leif by ordering him to throttle back on the hyper-engines.

'No need to give away any more of our capabilities than we have to,' their captain said. 'For all we know, contestants representing the other races could be checking us out in veeyar.' His white teeth appeared in a fierce grin. 'Let them think that last maneuver hurt us. We might be able to surprise them in the real race.'

The real race. It took a second for David's words to sink in as Leif followed his orders. A moment later, they were surrounded by the gentle flow of a million-mile-long ionization field.

That was the finish line! They'd won!

Andy whooped in triumph. Matt yelled, 'All right!'

David simply sat very still in the command seat of the ship he'd designed.

They came to a stop, and the viewscreen's image shifted. Lon Corben, the Pinnacle Productions publicity exec who'd been running the contestant search, smiled out at them. During the briefing for the mock race, he'd appeared in the uniform of a Federation Fleet Admiral. But now he was all business, wearing the 'Californian casual' business outfit of the entertainment industries.

Corben's open-necked shirt was a dazzling white – real linen from the looks of it, Leif thought. It must have cost a fortune. The executive's brocade vest had the sheen of real silk as well. In a world where more and more agriculture had to be devoted to food production, organic fibers were the ultimate status symbol.

'Congratulations to the crew of the—' Corben's eyes flicked to an off-image display. '*Onrust*. I'm pleased to announce that you've won the final elimination round for Galactic Federation contestants, and will represent the Federation in the upcoming Great Race.'

He gave the Net Force Explorers a wide, if synthetic, smile. The guy's slick, Leif thought. But then, most executive types were.

'My assistant will be in touch with you all regarding schedules and accommodations for the actual race. Again, my congratulations on a job very well done.'

Corben cut his connection – and so did the Net Force Explorers. They dropped out of veeyar – and into the computer suite of the Anderson's Washington apartment. Leif had come down to D.C. for the elimination trials. His father had offered the use of his cutting-edge systems for their command post. Leif could just as easy have telecommuted in on veeyar, but he thought there was a morale advantage to actually being all together.

Maybe that was just an illusion, but it seemed to have paid off.

Andy hopped out of his computer-link couch. 'We did it! We're on our way to California! Land of sun, beach-babes—'

'Smog, and earthquakes,' David finished. 'Those Pacific Coast simulations you like so much aren't exactly like the real thing.'

'Tell me about it,' Matt said with a laugh. 'In the sims, Andy always gets a tan.'

A blush crept across Andy's freckled cheeks. 'Come on, guys. Veeyar is the closest I've ever come to California. For any of us . . . except Leif.'

Now it was Leif's turn to be embarrassed. *That's me, the rich kid*, he thought.

'California? It's easy,' he said. 'Just think of it as a weird, alien world . . . with the capital of weirdness located in Hollywood.'

The boys laughed.

'I think Dad ordered some supplies for the fridge,' Leif went on. 'Just in case we had reason for a celebration.'

'That's just what we should do,' David said.

'You got it!' Andy chimed in. He threw an arm around Matt and David's shoulders. 'We're boldly going to Planet California!'

Chapter Four

The limo was about middle-of-the-line, Leif estimated. On business junkets with his father, he'd seen better, he'd seen worse. He knew his friends probably hadn't seen anything like it, except in a sim.

David, Matt, and Andy sat with their eyes glued to the tinted windows, taking in the real southern California landscape. Summertime especially underlined the area's never-ending battle between humans and nature. Where there was money, there was water, greenery . . . and the gardeners to tend it. Without the intervention of human taste and plumbing, however, the land quickly reverted to its true state – arid semi-desert.

He didn't point this out to the others – why ruin the trip of their lives?

Leif and his friends weren't exactly suffering from jet lag, but he felt a certain travel fatigue. They'd traveled in the cramped coach seats on a regular jet instead of a space-plane. With the growth in veeyar, many people took virtual vacations these days – featuring all the fun of real travel, without the bugs, sunburns, cramped plane seats, flight delays, cancellations, and other unfortunate details that could make a real-world trip a less than perfect experience. Tourism and travel in coach class had suffered as a result – many of the old perks for the masses had disappeared as people had abandoned the real world of travel for the virtual life. Travel in first class was different – you could always get luxury if you were prepared to pay for it. But this trip was on the studio's nickel, and coach was the order of the day. Leif was tired and achy after spending hours jammed into an uncomfortable seat. He was ready for a hot shower and a chance to sack out as soon as he got into his hotel room.

Instead, they were going directly to the offices of Pinnacle Productions for more publicity. The limo pulled up in front of the office building, where a swarm of newspeople awaited the press conference.

'Just like an old-time awards show,' Leif murmured as they stepped out.

Nobody much bothered with them, except for a couple of reporters who asked the boys about their chances in the upcoming race.

David shrugged. 'Can't tell you our chances until I see how the competition shapes up.' A public-relations flunky went on about how excited everyone felt about coming to California. Leif was glad he'd remembered to bring sunglasses.

Another limo pulled up, and the boys were immediately forgotten as more famous prey for the reporters emerged. Nils Olsen, the actor who played Captain Venn, faced the cameras and recorders, a quick, almost shy smile flitting across his chiseled, regular features. In jeans and an open-necked sweater, he seemed very different from the stern, commanding figure in the fitted tunic of a Federation Fleet Captain.

'Captain! Are you rooting for any particular team?'

Another fleeting smile appeared on his face. 'Rooting? I

haven't even met them yet.' His English was perfect American standard, with the faintest lilt of a Swedish accent.

The schools over there do really well with their foreign languages, Leif thought.

Olsen went on. 'But since you asked for the captain's reaction, of course he'd cheer for the Galactic federation's team.'

Huh! Leif thought. He almost sounds a bit nervous when he's not working from a script.

'Is it true that you're afraid of being typecast as Captain Venn? That your agent is fielding offers from other producers to do feature-length holos?' another reporter asked.

Leif braced himself for the patented Captain Venn thunderous reply. Instead, Nils Olsen merely rolled his eyes and shrugged. 'I think that's a "no comment" sort of question. Any other answer would end up getting me in trouble somehow.'

He abruptly headed down the narrow aisle between the media types, and the boys were shepherded after him. They entered the building and headed down halls to a large auditorium, still called a 'screening room' although flatscreen projection had been a dead technology for almost twenty years.

A holographic image of the *Ultimate Frontier* logo floated over the stage, where a good-sized crowd of people were already gathered.

Nils Olsen walked over to shake hands with a short, heavyset man with a full beard and long hair. Beside him was a familiar face.

'Lance Snowdon,' Matt muttered as they came closer. 'I hope we get some pictures with him. Catie would croak if

31

she thought we were hanging around with Commander Dominic!'

Catie Murray was another Net Force Explorer, a girl who had turned down David's invitation to crew the Mars expedition – and so had lost out on the *Ultimate Frontier* competition. Her refusal had led to Leif joining the crew.

The publicity person who'd met them at the airport brought the boys up to the heavyset bearded man. 'Mr Wallenstein, this is the group from Washington – the Galactic Federation's entry in the Great Race!'

Leif recognized the name he'd seen in the credits after every episode. Milos Wallenstein was the associate producer and script supervisor for *Ultimate Frontier*, the day-to-day head of things on the set. He looked like a throwback to an earlier style of Hollywood honcho in his neon-green blazer and black silk shirt.

'Welcome aboard,' he said in a raspy voice. 'Or maybe I should leave that to the captain. I can promise you an interesting couple of weeks, and maybe even some fun in between shooting the race sequences. I know I speak for all of the *Ultimate Frontier* cast and crew in greeting you.' The producer glanced over at Lance Snowdon. 'But I'm sure you'd be happier to meet some of the more famous faces.'

Snowdon came over to shake hands, an easy grin on his handsome face. With his cloud of curly hair and Vandyke beard, all he needed was a gold hoop earring to look like a pirate.

Matt eagerly stepped forward to shake hands, then blinked in astonishment. The show's action hero was barely taller than he was!

'I'm sure you guys will give this race everything you've got,' Snowdon said heartily. 'After all, the whole world is watching – or maybe I should say, the whole universe.'

'Thanks,' David said as he took the actor's hand. 'That makes us feel much better.'

His comeback was quick, but somehow, it just seemed to bounce off Snowdon's personality.

What is it about some people, Leif wondered, *that just standing beside them makes you look like a nerd?*

There was David, in his best clothes, his prized laptop computer slung over his shoulder . . . and Snowdon made him look like he'd just fallen off the turnip truck from Nowheresville.

Leif was sure he didn't look any better.

Ah, the magic of Hollywood, he thought.

As the last of the boys shook hands with Lance Snowdon, Wallenstein brought over Nils Olsen. The captain's words were brief and to the point. 'Good luck.' At least his now-you-see-it, now-you-don't smile seemed genuine.

While Olsen was shaking hands, a petite Asian woman came over and gave him a big smooch. 'I thought you weren't going to show up, Cap!' she said irreverently.

'I came in after the last racers here,' Olsen replied, gesturing to Leif and the others.

'Yu-Ying Cheang,' she introduced herself with a smile.

David gawked. 'C-Commander Konn?' he stuttered.

The woman bared her teeth in a laughing grimace and said in a guttural voice, 'Recognize me now, Soft Meat?'

That was the voice of Konn, but Leif's mental picture of the *Constellation*'s Drakieran combat commander was at least a head taller – and covered in armored scales.

Luckily, Ms Cheang seemed to take the boys' reaction in stride. 'See, Nils? You worry about being typecast as a star-cruiser captain. But me? Nobody even knows what I look like under all that makeup and prosthetic equipment.'

Olsen smiled down at his costar. 'Yu-Ying is a martial

arts champion who does all her own stunts.'

'Not anymore,' Yu-Ying interrupted. 'About a month ago, I fell and broke my tail.'

Andy, who had just been taking in all the Hollywood by-play, looked flustered. 'You seem—' he began, looking behind the actress.

Yu-Ying let off a loud crack of laughter. 'Commander Konn's tail!' The dragonlike alien warrior had an armored, prehensile tail that was as dangerous as another arm in hand-to-hand combat.

'I broke the prosthetic tail they glue onto my costume for the fighting sequences,' she explained. 'Now it won't work, which is why they brought in Pretty-boy Dominic to mix it up in that diplomatic-zoo episode.'

The young woman's eyes were wicked as she added, 'Personally, I got off with just a couple of bruises in a place I don't normally show in public.'

Olsen chuckled, taking in the Net Force Explorers' glazed expressions. 'I hope you're not too horrified to discover that the Federation Fleet's heroes have such feet of clay,' he said.

'Or such checkered pasts,' a white-haired woman said, coming up to them. 'At least Yu-Ying appears on screen, even if it's under a ton of goop. I only come on as a voice.'

'Of course,' Leif said. 'You're Rebecca Lorne, the voice of Soma.' Fans loved the Nimboid energy-being who served as the *Constellation*'s resident Contact Officer and ambassador, but the character was actually a hologram. Here was the woman whose voice gave the image its personality and charm. Rebecca Lorne was a handsome older woman wearing a classic white linen suit.

'Is it a problem, acting with a hologram?' Matt asked.

Olsen smiled. 'More a matter of timing things correctly.

The image is preprogrammed, so you have to be ready to react to its movements.'

'And not walk into it – as some captains have been known to do,' Yu-Ying joked.

'You kids have it easy,' Rebecca scoffed. 'When I played Marian in *Kong 2001*, the special effects went in *after* the scene was shot. All I had to work with was a big sheet of poster paper with an X taped on it to tell me where the monster's head was.

Leif tried not to gawk. The old flatscreen film had spawned a famous image – a beautiful blond woman in a torn, filmy nightgown cringing away from the giant ape's poking finger.

'Yeah, that was me,' Rebecca told him, a wry grin relaxing her features into a shadow of that long-ago image. 'I was quite the fox in those days, even if I say so myself. The baddest girl in the soaps, twenty-five years ago.'

'Before holos,' Yu-Ying teased.

'Before holos,' Rebecca agreed, 'and all those "what you see is what you get" special effects.'

Wallenstein had been conferring with his publicity people. Now he came back. 'The press people will be joining us in a moment, so we'd better get things arranged.'

'Sure,' Rebecca Lorne said. 'Get 'em away from us, before we scar them for life!'

A publicity person beckoned to the Net Force Explorers, and Leif and the boys followed. Technicians were suddenly swarming over the stage, moving groups of people – the other teams, Leif realized – to premarked spots. A quartet of solemn-looking young men as dark as David, in the embroidered neckcloth shirts fashionable in the African republics, were led into place – and the image of a Setangi warrior popped into existence beside them.

Two pairs of boys and girls, blond and apple-cheeked, posed beside the image of a Laragant officer cadet. They were all chattering excitedly in a language that sounded familiar, though he was too far away to make out many of the words. Norwegian? No, Danish, Leif finally decided. Good. His Danish was getting rusty. It would be nice to have a chance to use it.

A young Federation Fleet cadet in the forest-green tunic of an Engineering trainee appeared off to the left of the stage.

'I guess that's where we should be headed,' Matt said.

David, however, had stopped dead in his tracks. 'Man!' The exclamation was almost like a curse. 'I see it, but I don't believe it.'

'What?' Leif asked.

'You weren't around when we were talking about it, but I bet you know the connection between the alien races on *Ultimate Frontier* and the international broadcast market.'

Leif nodded. 'You mean the way they boost ratings by having various nationalities and so on identify with the *Ultimate Frontier* races.' He frowned. 'What about it?'

David lowered his voice. 'Pinnacle Productions must have slanted the results of the racing trials. Look around! Black Africans race as the Setangis. A European team becomes the Laragants. Who represents the Galactic Federation? Who else but us all-American boys. It's like typecasting!'

'No way!' Andy objected. 'We kicked major butt in our races.'

'At least it looked that way,' Matt said slowly.

'And surprise, surprise! The right team for the American market won.' David's voice mixed suspicion and disgust. 'They're just using us for the publicity – to see if they can rake off a couple more ratings points.'

'Come on, guys,' Leif said. 'We pretty much knew going in that the whole idea of the contest was to beat the drums for *Ultimate Frontier*. That's why all the reporters are outside, waiting to get in.'

'Yeah, right,' Matt objected. 'But when we went in, we thought this was going to be a fair race.'

'We don't know that it's not,' Leif said. 'Maybe the producers skewed the results a little to get the competitors they wanted. But whatever they do now, they do in the full glare of publicity.'

'So?' David asked.

'So, we play the game – and keep our eyes open,' Leif said. 'I don't think Pinnacle would stick us with a team of ringers. Most of these kids just look excited to be here.'

'No!' a harsh voice cut across the excited babbling in the background.

Leif looked around. A hulking guy with slicked-back hair and a thick mustache loomed over an unhappy-looking technician.

'We will not stand where you want to put us,' Mr Mustache went on in a loud voice. He stabbed an angry finger at the Federation Fleet cadet and at the surprised-looking Danish kids. 'It is close to the warmongering Americans, and right beside the oppressors of the so-called European Union.'

Wallenstein came over at the sound of raised voices. 'Look here, Mr – ah—'

'Cetnik,' the mustached man declared. Leif nodded. Yes. There was a definite Mittel-European accent lurking under the guy's English.

'Mr Cetnik. When you agreed to participate—'

'We did not agree to be insulted!' Cetnik cut him off. 'I

am responsible for these young people, to their parents – and to my government.'

Leif followed the dramatically outflung arm. Four kids stood off to the side. They wore gray-green outfits that looked more like military uniforms than any school outfits Leif had ever seen. Three of them were guys with dark hair and sullen expressions. The last was a striking-looking blond girl with a face and figure that would turn eyes even in Hollywood. Beside them rose the holo-image of a silver-skinned humanoid alien whose face had no features – a Thurien.

Cetnik continued. 'The Carpathian Alliance expects us to represent them in the world – and we must demand the respect our nation deserves!'

Chapter Five

Wallenstein glanced indecisively toward the doors where the reporters would be entering in a moment. The producer dithered for a moment, sighed, and began talking to the technicians.

Then they began rearranging the teams.

Leif shook his head in disbelief. Why would a man in charge of one of the most lucrative holo-franchises in the world cave before a loudmouthed rep from a lunatic-fringe foreign government?

Frowning, he turned his head for a nice, long look at the mustached Mr Cetnik. Leif's dad had dealt with a lot of diplomats, and so had Leif. As representatives of their countries, diplomats could generally be described as 'smooth'. Cetnik, on the other hand, had shown he had lots of rough edges. He didn't look or sound very diplomatic.

The impression I get is that he's more like a security guy, Leif thought. *And in the Carpathian Alliance, that probably means secret police.*

Technicians worked furiously to refocus hologram images to please Cetnik and his team. Not too close to the Europeans, or the Americans, or the African team, given the Carpathian Alliance's weird racial theories.

At last they had an acceptable lineup, and the press was invited in. Leif just about turned off his brain while all the publicity hoopla went on. He was tired after the long flight. Mainly, he concentrated on not yawning in public.

One little ceremony brought him out of his stupor. Each team's captain was requested to step over to Milos Wallenstein. There they would hand over a software version of the ship they had designed. The racing craft would all be downloaded to Pinnacle Productions' computer system where the race would be run, checked to make sure that they matched the vehicles used in the preliminary rounds, and checked again to be sure they matched the specs that Pinnacle Productions had issued for the race.

If it's on the up and up, it means a level playing field for everyone racing, Leif thought. *If they're downloading everything so that they can control the outcome, well, that's the way it goes. If the studio's not going to keep the race fair, there's not much we can do about it unless things get pretty blatant. Besides, it will give the studio better control of the actual special effects for the episode. We'll look cooler in our moment of glory.*

He stiffened slightly as a new thought hit him. For some of the competitors, their creations would be running on a system considerably better than anything in their home countries.

The Carpathian Alliance, for instance, had been under strict technology embargoes ever since the last war.

Maybe that's why they're pushing so hard to win this race, Leif thought. Besides offering a moment of glory on *Ultimate Frontier,* Pinnacle Productions had promised all kinds of techno-toys for the winners, stuff that wouldn't even be available in the States for at least another year. And from the description of the computer setup in the prize package, the stuff really rocked.

Leif glanced thoughtfully in Cetnik's direction again. More than enough reason to send a secret policeman . . . or even an out-and-out spy.

As if he had read Leif's mind, the Carpathian representative stepped out to make another speech. 'Our friends of the free media are probably aware that the aggressors of the United States still pursue their war against the people of the Carpathian Alliance. Because of abusive trade restrictions, our team will be unable to bring the promised prizes back to the homeland in the event of our victory.'

He makes it sound like a foregone conclusion, Leif thought.

'Our response is simple – and global. Should the Alliance win, the technology will be shared with deserving groups around the world.'

The key word was *shared*, Leif suddenly realized. Cetnik and his junior goons might not be able to walk away with any hardware, but any hacker worth his salt could rip it apart and go back to the homeland with equipment and programming savvy two generations beyond anything currently in use there.

And they'd still get the propaganda value of giving the prizes away.

In spite of his dislike, Leif had to give them credit. These guys were dangerous – maybe even more dangerous than they looked.

At last, the publicity rituals were over, and the boys were finally free to head to their hotel. They were led out a different doorway, through the maze of Pinnacle Productions offices, and out through the rear exit of the building, where they found their limo waiting.

'I could get used to this,' David said as they pulled away

through the Los Angeles traffic.

Matt nodded. 'Beats an autobus.' Much of Washington's mass transit was handled by driverless, computer-controlled buses.

'I don't know,' Andy said. 'I think this is about the same size as a Washington bus.'

'You'll find lots of autobuses here,' the young publicist who was acting as their guide said. 'L.A. has worked hard to improve its mass-transit options – although the studio has arranged for rental cars for each team. You'll get the paperwork to fill out when we get to your hotel.'

'Where are we staying?' Leif asked the young woman.

'Casa Beverly Hills,' she answered, 'right on Rodeo Drive.'

'Yow!' Andy exclaimed.

Leif kept his mouth shut. He knew that Beverly Hills and Rodeo Drive had suffered a downturn since the earthquake of 2019. The trickle of movers and shakers who'd quietly been finding mansions in Connecticut and condos in New York City had become a flood. The rich and famous had decided it was more pleasant to live in places that didn't attempt to shake, slide, flood, or burn their houses down, and the expensive stores that served them had followed.

The increasing importance of the Net had also contributed to the decline. People had lived in Beverly Hills to be close to 'the industry' – whether that meant music, TV, or film. But the growing versatility of the Net had literally allowed people to 'dial in' performances. A big star could be anywhere on Earth – or up in one of the orbital habitats – all through rehearsals, and through the miracle of veeyar and holographic projection, still be 'on the set'.

There were even rumors that some very sought-after

actor types hadn't been physically present when their last performances had been lensed. They'd only 'been there' in holoform, either because they'd gotten fat or become paranoid recluses . . . or both.

Leif hoped his friends wouldn't expect to see big stars during their stay in Beverly Hills. What they'd see were tourists.

Still, he thought, *the Casa Beverly Hills makes a nice address for an out-of-towner.*

Pinnacle Productions hadn't splurged on the entertainment budget for their guests, but they'd been generous enough. The boys stepped from the elevator to an elaborate set of real-wood double doors, which opened to reveal a comfortable suite. The living room had a large window giving a view of what used to be some of the most expensive real estate in the U.S. of A. It was flanked on either side by bedrooms. They boys would double up, but as David said as he put his suitcase down, 'Just the living room's bigger than my whole house at home.'

The publicist left after taking care of the bellman, and the boys began exploring the suite. A tiny but working kitchen filled one corner of the living room – probably for business entertaining, Leif thought. But someone from Pinnacle Productions had been on the job. The small refrigerator was filled with a selection of soft drinks and juices, courtesy of the studio, and the cabinets had a wide assortment of snack foods.

'Man, I could use something to drink,' Andy said. 'I don't know if it was the plane or the weather out here, but my throat feels like somebody hung it out to dry in the sun.'

They all poured themselves glasses of soda, and flopped down on the overstuffed couch and chairs facing the living room window.

'Well, this has certainly been a day,' David said. 'I feel as if I wandered into a weird veeyar – or my own personal holofilm.'

Matt laughed. 'I know what you mean. Everything seems like make-believe – except for the weirdest flashes of real life.' He looked down at his hand. 'I can't believe I shook hands with Lance Snowdon.'

'I can't believe what a shrimp he turned out to be,' Andy cut in.

Matt nodded. 'Or that you could see right through his hair and down to his scalp.'

'Oh, I don't know,' Leif said. 'Fans of the series have always been arguing over which were better – the captains with hair, or the captains without.'

Andy hooted with laughter. 'Not to mention the captains with the cheap toupees.'

'You've given me a reason to hope that Commander Dominic gets promoted,' David chuckled. 'We'll see how things go for a captain who's losing his hair.'

'I've seen more behind-the-scenes stuff today that I'd find in a month on the Net.' Matt suddenly stifled a yawn. 'And all I want to do is sleep.'

'Tell me about it,' Andy said. He hopped to his feet. 'Come on, bunkie. Let's find out if the beds in this dump are as comfortable as that couch.'

The sitting room got quieter as the two boys went off to claim one of the bedchambers. David sat back on the couch, finishing off his glass of soda. Then he opened the bag that still hung from his shoulder and took out his laptop computer.

Technically speaking, the portable unit was obsolete – its business niche had been taken over by palm-sized digital assistants that responded to spoken orders instead of a keyboard or a screen interface.

Leif's father had invested in a company that thought it could bring the laptop market back. The laptops were as fast and as powerful as the console computers that everybody used on the Net, after all. They just lacked the interfaces and systems contained in compulink chairs that made long-term veeyar interactions possible. It had been one of Dad's few bad calls. Almost nobody had bought them. Leif had helped his father unload some of the inventory by arranging a very favorable price for any Net Force Explorers who wanted to purchase them.

David had gone for the deal. After all, the unit he was working on now had the same capability as the compulink system in his apartment – or better.

'No regrets about buying the old clunker?' Leif asked his friend.

'It may seem like a clunker to you,' David said, peering down at the spaceship design projected by the laptop's display. 'But it's everything I hoped for – and more.'

He glanced at Leif. 'You know, this is something you don't see anymore. It's the first pure computer system I ever owned. My family's machine is tied in with all the apartment's electronics. The stuff I learned on in school is hardwired into the Net. Most handheld equipment is multipurpose, like a wallet phone that acts like a computer only after you hook into the Net and draw upon Net resources.'

David patted the little box on his lap. 'But this sucker is really *my* computer unless and until I physically connect it to the rest of the world.'

'The hotel is completely hardwired – its system is probably bigger and faster,' Leif pointed out. 'There's a port over there where you could download all your files. At least you'd get a better display and not have to worry about going blind.'

'No, I'd just have to worry about getting hacked,' David replied.

Leif laughed. 'Some wild-eyed Frontie fan who wants to know everything there is to know about the competing ships? Or maybe a bookmaker who wants the ships' specs so he can figure the odds he'll offer the bettors?'

'Try some of the other contestants – like that weird crew from the Carpathian Alliance,' David replied.

Reluctantly, Leif nodded. 'You might have a point there. If not the crew, that Mr Cetnik might make a stab at it – although from the looks of him, the most complicated piece of machinery he ever operated was a submachine gun.'

'Looks can be deceiving,' David said. 'Especially in the C.A.' He rolled his eyes. 'Those people are *crazy*, Anderson. Did you see those kids there today? They're wearing the uniform of the national schools. Change the buttons and add a few insignia, and it's identical with the uniform for the Alliance army.'

Leif shrugged. 'Guess it saves them money.'

David shook his head. 'It's the way they think. The Carpathian Alliance literally considers itself a nation at arms. Everybody in the country can be called upon to repel invaders. They have courses about it in the schools. The kids are dressed like soldiers because that's how the government intends to use them, fighting up close and personal.'

He pursed his lips as if he'd tasted something bad. 'They teach those kids that the United States is the greatest cause of evil in the world today. And then, of course, there's something I find personally offensive – their screwball

46

racial theories. You know how philologists have been studying the ancient Indo-European language?'

Leif nodded again. Research had been going on since the 1700s, when a British official in India had noticed similarities between ancient Sanskrit words and words meaning the same things in Latin and Greek – basic vocabulary, like the words for 'father' and 'water'.

'Indo-European' was the name given to this root tongue, whose descendant languages were spoken across the old countries of two continents . . . and in new countries across the globe. In recent decades, however, scientists had attempted to probe the roots of Indo-European, trying to find out where the language had originated.

Using computers, they'd exhaustively compared words in various languages, noting what matched – and what didn't. For instance, words connected to water showed the same ancient roots. So did the words about rivers. But the ancient languages – and the modern ones – came up with different names for seas. That would indicate that the original Indo-Europeans lived inland, away from any large bodies of water. Further clues had narrowed down the possible area – things like the names of trees and animals that all the vocabularies shared.

'They finally narrowed down the area where it was first spoken to southern Poland, right?' Leif asked.

David nodded. 'And you must know that there's another name for the people who spoke Indo-European – Aryans.'

Leif didn't say anything. The name had been seized upon by too many people pushing theories about a 'master race,' explaining the success of nineteenth-century Europe in carving out colonial empires in terms of 'Aryan heritage' instead of superior technology and finance.

One theorist – a guy named Adolf Hitler – had not

only praised Aryan supremacy, but had written about the need to reduce, even exterminate, what he called 'lesser races.'

He'd put the world through decades of horror when he tried to put his theories into action. And ever since then, groups had seized on the word 'Aryan' to justify their racism.

David went on. 'Anyway, our friends from the Carpathians cooked up a neat theory. Since Indo-European was first spoken on Polish territory, that means that the Slavic races – which happens to include the people from the C.A. – are the true Aryans!'

Leif blinked. 'Wait a minute. The Aryans – Indo-Europeans – whatever you want to call them, they date back to about five thousand years ago. The Slavs enter the historical record about fifteen hundred years ago. That's a pretty big time gap – a lot of people marched through that territory in the meantime.'

'It's a nonsensical claim,' David agreed. 'But the Carpathian Alliance is pushing it hard.'

'And the Nazis – Hitler's Aryans – they slaughtered lots of Slavs for belonging to a so-called inferior race.'

'According to the C.A. party line, Hitler was a false prophet who stole his ideas.' David tapped the side of his head. 'These people are wacko, Anderson. Dangerously wacko.'

'Where did you find out all this stuff?' Leif asked.

'I talked with Captain Winters. He spent some time over there – and he likes to know the enemy.' David looked grim. 'So do I. Those Alliance zombies are in this contest for the propaganda value. They want to win the Great Race – to show that they're the *greatest* race.'

Leif stepped over to the window. 'That's a reasonable

motive under the circumstances, I suppose,' he said. 'I can think of others—'

His voice cut off, and he squinted. Their room was in the center of the hotel, overlooking Rodeo Drive with the mountains in the distance. But the H-shaped building had two wings that jutted out on either side. And Leif had noticed something odd in one of the windows over-looking theirs.

It was an antenna, an old-fashioned rig like the satellite dishes people once used to catch world broadcasts in the days before the Net became the delivery system of choice.

There was no need for a direct-feed link in a hotel already hardwired for every sort of communications, unless somebody wanted a really secure connection. It was aimed downward – right at their room!

Chapter Six

'Hey, David,' Leif said, fighting to keep his voice even and his expression bored. 'Why don't you turn that thing off for a moment and come check out the view?'

'Leif, I'm running simulations, trying to get a handle to all the possible quirks and surprises we might come across trying to race the *Onrust*.' David's eyes were still glued to the display from his laptop computer. 'It's hard enough being captain of this pocket rocket without—'

He bit off his words, but Leif could just as easily imagine what would have followed. Something along the lines of, 'Without being bothered by your idiot interruptions.'

Leif turned from the window. 'I think you ought to come over here. *Now*.'

David caught the note of warning in his friend's tone and set the computer aside. 'All right,' he said, rising from the couch. 'What's the big deal?'

'I want you to see something,' Leif said, gesturing off to the horizon. 'Keep your face pointing straight ahead, but move your eyes to the right. Up three floors, the seventh window from where the west wing juts out. No!' he abruptly warned. 'Don't actually turn and look. Just move your eyes.'

David drew an annoyed breath as he followed Leif's instructions. But whatever he was going to say passed in a quick outrush of air.

'There's something in the window,' he finally whispered.

'An antenna,' Leif agreed, his voice equally low. He didn't think that whoever was over there had eavesdropping equipment, but he couldn't be sure. They were quite possibly under observation – that was why he kept up the charade of 'enjoying' the view.

'People sort of forget it these days, since entertainment, voice, and data communications all route through the Net, but computers – including that laptop over there – throw off radio-frequency radiation.'

'My dad mentioned that,' David said. 'When he was a kid, the family's flatscreen TV would sometimes pick up images from the display – the CRT – when the computer was on at the same time. Word-processing pages, or the screen of some game his brother was playing.'

'Was the TV on cable or an aerial?' Leif asked.

'I never quite understood what he was talking about,' David admitted. 'Dad always talked about rabbit ears.'

'That was a kind of antenna,' Leif said. 'But the dish sticking out that window there is much more sensitive. I'm sure it would have no problem picking up enough leaked radiation to duplicate whatever's on your display.'

David jerked as if he'd been stabbed. 'Those miserable, scum-sucking – I think I'm going to go up there and kick some butt!'

He stalked away from the window, but Leif quickly intercepted him.

'No, you're not,' Leif said. 'I'm the one who's supposed to have the temper around here.' He pointed to his red hair. 'We don't want to give whoever's up there any hint that we know what's going on . . . not until we can nail them.'

Leif nodded toward David's laptop. 'What you're going to do is call up an image of the *Onrust* – something non-sensitive – and fool around with it, tweak it, to keep our spy upstairs interested – and staying in place. Meanwhile, I'll lead a small delegation downstairs to have a chat with the management.'

David glared at him – he really wanted to get his hands on that snoop in the window.

'Look, they've seen you with the laptop – and they've seen you working on it. If I start fooling around on it, they might get suspicious and pull the plug. Besides, I don't know which files might tell them something dangerous, and which are just pretty pictures.'

Grudgingly, David nodded. 'I've got an earlier version in one of the directories – completely different specs from the file we turned in. I can start taking that to pieces—'

'Good,' Leif said. 'Keep them on the edge of their seats.' While David returned to his computer, Leif left the room.

One bedroom still had its door open. The other was closed. Leif quietly slid the closed door open and stepped into semi-darkness. Matt and Andy had simply closed the shades and flaked out, fully dressed, on their beds.

Just looking at the sleeping boys made Leif's eyes feel gritty. He stifled a yawn. This was what *he* should be doing. But no, he had to go and spot the spy in the sky. Or at least the spy in the upstairs window.

Leif decided against waking both of his friends. Matt would look sturdy and dependable if they went to talk to the manager. Andy would probably mouth off and annoy whoever was in charge. Stepping around Andy's bed, Leif leaned over Matt. He put his hand over the sleeping boy's mouth and pinched his nose shut between thumb and forefinger.

Having his air cut off quickly roused Matt to wakefulness. His eyes popped open, and he made some sort of sound, which was muffled by the hand at his mouth. Then he stared at Leif.

'We've got a little trouble,' Leif whispered in Matt's ear. 'Spiff yourself up. We're going to go and see the manager.'

He headed for the door as Matt silently got off the bed and followed him.

In the bathroom, Leif filled Matt in on what he'd noticed while the other boy ran a cold washcloth over his face and combed his hair. The Leif made himself a little more presentable and they went downstairs to the front desk.

The clerk was surprised when they asked to see the manager – and even more surprised when they refused to tell him what it was about. But the boys' perseverance paid off. In the end, they wound up with an assistant manager. Her name was Ms Ramirez. She was an olive-skinned, dark-haired, businesslike young woman in a quiet suit instead of the blue blazers and gray slacks most of the hotel staff seemed to wear.

She frowned as Leif explained what he'd seen in the window overlooking theirs – and how it could be used. 'We don't get much trouble on the premises,' she said.

Leif said nothing. Perhaps in the old days, when more people from the entertainment business stayed here, there might have been worries about corporate espionage. With tourists, the concerns were more with theft and pilfering.

Ms Ramirez looked at Matt. 'Did you see this antenna, or dish, or whatever it was?'

Leif was glad he'd brought along his all-American, reliable-looking friend.

Matt nodded. 'I only took a quick look between the curtains – we didn't want to warn whoever was up there. But I saw something aimed at our living room window.'

'And where did you say this was?' The assistant manager turned back to Leif.

'Three floors above us – on the fifth floor,' Leif replied. 'Seven windows out into the west wing.'

'There are five hundred rooms in this hotel, not to mention ninety suites,' Ms Ramirez said. 'Computer,' she ordered the unit in her desk. 'Floor plan for west wing, fifth floor. Highlight the room with the seventh window in the southern exposure.'

'Processing,' a smooth voice seemed to announce from thin air. 'Location pinpointed.'

'Display,' the young woman ordered.

A hologram swam into existence over the desk. It showed an architect's floor plan for the west wing of the hotel. It wasn't a case of one window per room. Some of the windows were paired, as they were in the boys' suite. One location was highlighted with a glaring red glow.

'What room is that?' Ms Ramirez asked.

'Room 568,' the computer replied.

'And who is checked in there?' the assistance manager went on.

'Processing.' The computer took a moment to check the front desk's registration records.

It seemed almost hesitant as it reported. 'Room 568 has been vacant for the past two days.'

That got Ms Ramirez's attention. 'Perhaps a previous guest just left something in the window,' she suggested. But her tone of voice insinuated that she didn't believe her own explanation. 'Let's have a chat with Hotel Security and check into this.'

In hologram crime dramas, house detectives usually were fat, badly dressed incompetents who'd been thrown out of the police force and walked around chewing half-smoked cigars.

In traveling with his dad, however, Leif had stayed in plenty of upscale hotels – places that took and interest in protecting their wealthy and powerful guests. He'd met many hotel security officers, and the man escorting them and the assistant manager fit the type. He had neatly trimmed hair worn in the current corporate style, wore a blue blazer like everyone else working at the Casa Beverly Hills – and there wasn't a trace of a cigar around him.

He had a wide chest, and muscles bunched in his arms under the blazer sleeves.

Their elevator reached the fifth floor, and the security man in the blue blazer led the way down the hall.

Security, Leif thought, an irreverent notion tickling his brain. *At least he's not wearing a red tunic*.

He shook his head. He had *Ultimate Frontier* on the brain these days.

They arrived at the door to Room 568. 'Please stay back,' the man warned the people accompanying him.

He reached into his jacket. Leif saw Matt staring avidly, as if he expected the guy to pull out a gun and kick in the door.

Poor Matt was in for a disappointment. The security man produced the house compukey and pressed it to the lock. Instantly, the door swung open.

Room 568 was designed for a single traveler. It was much smaller than either of the bedrooms in the Net

Force Explorers' suite. Even the bed was skinnier. The door to the bathroom was open, and so was the closet.

It took about three seconds to make sure that the place was empty.

The assistant manager turned to the boys with a stern expression on her face. 'If you've been wasting our time—' she threatened.

But her security officer was prowling the room, looking in the wastepaper basket, the bathroom sink, and the toilet. 'No, someone was in here, ma'am,' he said.

'How do you know, Harris?' Ms Ramirez demanded.

'This is the non-smoking wing,' the security man replied. 'No one is supposed to bring any smoking materials in here.' He sniffed the air. 'But you can tell there was *some* kind of smoke in here very recently.' His nose wrinkled. 'Or at least that someone set fire to something.'

Leif took a deep breath and nodded. 'Somebody *was* smoking,' he said. 'And it wasn't American tobacco.' The smell was rougher than the usual cigarette smoke, spicier – somehow more exotic. Leif had encountered it before on trips with his father. 'That's Turkish tobacco.'

A smile tugged at his lips when he saw the looks he was getting from the other people in the room. 'Believe me, I'm no Sherlock Holmes. I don't have a database of hundreds of kinds of cigarette ash. But I have traveled with my dad through the parts of Europe and the Middle East where they smoke this stuff. Over here, you usually find the stuff in pipe tobacco mixtures.'

The harsh scent in the air didn't seem to remind Leif of pipe smoke, however. It brought to mind the image of office lobbies in certain European cities – places where public smoking was still tolerated. A memory suddenly clicked in Leif's mind. They'd been in Hungary – an office building in Budapest. His dad had had business to transact there.

They'd passed a janitor who was smoking a villainous-looking cheap cigarette. Leif had coughed his head off, almost choked from the fumes. Mr Anderson had simply shaken his head. 'Ten-percent Turkish, ninety-percent rags.'

A cheap cigarette with some Turkish tobacco and lots of additives – the kind sold in Eastern Europe, the Balkans, where you found Hungary . . .

And the Carpathian Alliance.

Ms Ramirez wasn't wondering about Turkish tobacco. The assistant manager was more worried about what an intruder meant to the reputation of her hotel.

'Harris, are you telling me that someone broke in here—' she began.

The security officer shook his head, almost a sad gesture. 'I don't think that's the way it worked out, Ms Ramirez. Whoever was in here, they probably got in with a house compukey. Looks like we'll have to question the day people. Cleaning workers, the bell staff . . .'

When they knew to start looking, they didn't have to search very far. Security people and the managers began questioning the staff members. One of the bellmen started looking shifty as soon as he heard the words 'Room 568'.

'Oswald!' Ms Ramirez frowned furiously. 'Did you let an unauthorized person into one of our rooms?'

The bellman wasn't all that much older than Leif or Matt. His face was now beaded with sweat. 'I – uh—' he stammered.

Harris, the security man, sighed. 'What story did he hand you?' he asked.

Oswald looked at his shoes. 'He said he was a detective. Wanted a room there so he could take some pictures and get the goods on somebody.'

'Did you get a name? What did he look like?' Harris kept trying. It might be closing the barn door after the horse was gone, but the security operative wanted to make sure that the spy wouldn't get back into the hotel again.

But the young bellman could only shrug his shoulders. 'I barely looked at his face,' he said, 'only at the bills he was holding out. Cash money.'

Sure, Leif thought. *Working in a fading tourist hotel wouldn't bring a lot of cash his way. Nowadays, guests even put tips for the staff on their credit cards.*

'Come on, Oswald,' Harris pressed. 'You had to notice *something.*'

Oswald shook his head, then stopped. 'The guy talked . . . funny. Like a foreigner. That's all I noticed. That's all I can say.'

So, Leif thought, *I was right! Somebody really is spying on us!*

Chapter Seven

Leif felt tired and grouchy as the boys sat down to dinner. He'd tried out his bed after his little stint of playing detective, but even though he'd closed his eyes, he hadn't been able to sleep. Too many questions kept bouncing around in his skull.

Who had been spying on them? Cetnik? Somebody else? Whoever it was, they must have penetrated the hotel's computer system. Leif was sure he and his fellow Net Force Explorers hadn't tipped off the electronic eavesdropper. Yet the spy had known in advance that they were on their way – and had gotten out of Room 568.

Probably the warning had gone out when Ms Ramirez tried to locate the room or checked the register. All it would take was an inserted hang-and-terminate program to pass the alert and erase itself.

Any really good programmer could pull that trick. David could do it. Maybe even Matt and Andy. Which meant that the surveillance wasn't necessarily official. A team member – or a whole team – could have been scouting out the opposition.

Using the receiver dish wasn't exactly high-tech either. In fact, it was trailing-edge technology, using something that most people would consider obsolete.

But then, people had to make do with lots of old-fashioned technology in the Carpathian Alliance. The international embargoes kept new systems out of the country – folks in the C.A. had to use computers that had long ago gone to the scrap heap in other parts of the world.

The problem was, Leif was left with a tantalizing set of clues, but no hard indication to tell *who* was after them.

After getting up and heading to the hotel restaurant for dinner, the boys resumed their discussion over whodunnit.

'It's that Cetnik guy,' Matt said after they'd put in their orders. 'We saw already that he doesn't mind throwing his weight around. Spying on us might give his team a crucial leg up . . . and win the race for the glory of the Carpathian Alliance.'

'And cause an international incident if he got caught?' David shook his head. 'The more I think about it, the more the whole thing looks like a stupid prank. It's the sort of thing a kid might pull off, not an adult who had something to lose.'

'If you think it's a kid, what about the cigarette smoke?' Andy asked.

David looked at him. 'Like you've never met a kid who has tried the wicked weed? If a kid is naughty enough to spy on his – or her – competitors, the kid is naughty enough to smoke.'

'And stunt their growth,' Matt added with a grin, parroting a warning that had to be a hundred years old by now.

'On the other hand, whoever it was had surveillance in place, was warned by it, and got away. An amateur probably wouldn't have thought of that, even if it was in his capabilities to do the programming. That gives the operation a professional flavor,' Leif said. 'That brings us back to Mr Cetnik – or some other agent of the C.A. The Alliance considers the U.S. to be a major enemy. They must have spies in place.'

Andy hooted with laughter. 'Comrade, you must stop zee evil American warmongers from winning zis race on der holonet!' he hissed in a thick Mittel-European accent. 'Yawohl!' He glanced around the table. 'Or whatever they say in Whatzislavia. It's a stupid holo show, Leif. I don't see why you have to drag spies and stuff into it.'

'Not counting the propaganda value of winning a race on a "stupid holo show" that appears all over the world, there's the question of the prizes,' Leif answered. 'Pinnacle Productions is offering all sorts of computer stuff—'

'Which the C.A. zookeeper said they would give away if they won,' David pointed out.

'Right,' Leif responded. 'But I'm sure they'd have to "evaluate" it before they give the stuff away to all those deserving groups. If you were doing that job, how much embargoed technology would you be able to carry off in your head?'

David closed his mouth with a snap.

'I also hear that the winners will get some simulation time on the LM-2025,' Leif went on. 'That's the hottest system in the world right now. Getting into the guts of a machine like that would tell a good technician a lot about the latest computer design.'

Matt nodded. 'And what's to stop them from calling up all sorts of other designs in veeyar? Even stuff that we'd consider hopelessly over the hill could jump-start their technology ahead by decades.'

David frowned. 'They're forced to make their own computer chips because of the embargo,' he said. 'Getting a look at a modern chip design *would* be a big help.'

'Okay, so there's a more grown-up motive for spying on us,' Andy said.

'And there's the fact that the hotel system was penetrated and rigged to provide a warning if their listening post was threatened,' Leif went on.

'We don't know that,' David objected. 'The hotel people didn't say anything about a security breach.'

'As if any hotel is going to admit that,' Andy said.

Matt nodded. 'From what I saw of that Ms Ramirez, I think they'd prefer to sweep the whole thing under the rug.'

'And we still don't know that *we* didn't somehow scare them off.' Andy put a hand on his chest and a virtuous expression on his face. 'Well, I know *I* didn't. I was asleep. But the rest of you guys – maybe they had the room bugged, or were bouncing a laser off the window glass to pick up what you were saying.' He gave them a wry grin. 'I don't know. Maybe whoever was up there could read lips.'

Leif let his breath out in a long sigh. Anything was possible. Maybe his whole effort to catch the spy had been doomed from the beginning. There didn't seem much sense talking about it. They just went in circles, spinning off more and wilder theories.

Matt frowned. 'You think we should tell Captain Winters about this?' he asked. 'After all, it could be a plot to steal prohibited technology.'

His suggestion brought another sigh from Leif, who'd been kicking the same idea around during his sleepless time on the hotel-room bed. 'I don't think we've got enough for him to justify any action,' he said. 'Do you really want to ask him to activate a Net Force team over something that may turn out to be a teenage prank?'

The sudden silence around the table was as much of an answer as that question needed.

'Maybe we don't know *who* put us under surveillance,' David finally spoke up. His face was grim. 'But we know for sure it *did* happen. Tomorrow morning, I'm going to go to the head honcho – Wallenstein – and tell him all about it. The least we can do is rattle some cages.'

Andy nodded enthusiastically. 'Yeah! We can shake things up a little. If we keep quiet, the spy can just hunker down as if nothing happened. But if we stir things up, they'll have to react.' He grinned. 'And maybe, just maybe, they'll make a mistake and we can catch them.'

The waiter came with a large tray. Leif sniffed appreciatively. Real food, not the mass-processed soybean mockmeat that somehow always left a fish-oil flavor on the tongue.

Diverted from their conversation, the boys grabbed knives and forks for something they *could* deal with.

The publicist from Pinnacle Productions, Jane Givens, came to pick the Net Force Explorers up early the next morning. 'We have a pretty full schedule today,' she announced. 'There's a studio tour, including a visit to the *Ultimate Frontier* permanent sets.' The young woman made it sound as if that were a privilege not too many visitors were allowed. 'Followed by a luncheon, arrangements for your team's rental car, and then we'll see how your ship designs look on our computers—'

'I didn't want to say anything yesterday,' David said, 'but none of us is eighteen yet. I don't think it would be legal for any of us—' Washington, D.C., didn't allow anyone under the age of eighteen to apply for a driver's license without a special waiver, and very few of those waivers were granted.

'Do any of you have a license?' the publicist asked.

'I do,' Leif volunteered. He'd taken his road test at the age of sixteen, which was legal in New York State, although he still wasn't allowed to drive in New York City.

'And you're at least sixteen years old?'

Leif nodded.

'Then there should be no problem. Here in California, the legislature passed statewide approval for licensed drivers sixteen and up last year.' She shook her head. 'Don't thank me. Thank the anarcho-libertarians.'

'The whoozy-watzians?' Andy said.

'You mean you've been in California a full day and haven't heard the gospel according to Derle?' The young publicist seemed almost surprised. 'He's got ads on every holo-net and radio broadcast.'

'I guess we haven't bothered with either,' David said.

'Mainly we slept, ate, and then slept again,' Andy explained.

'Well, you'll encounter the propaganda machine sooner or later,' the young woman said. 'Elrod Derle is a million-aire, the kind we grow especially well here in California – eccentric. After making a pile in computers, he went into politics. Set up his own party, fighting for individual liberty against what he calls "the government rules monopoly".'

Leif blinked. 'Isn't that what all the political parties are saying?'

The woman laughed and shook her head again. 'But Derle and his anarcho-libertarians are trying to do some-thing about it. "Free intelligent people from the toils of micro-management." That's the way they put it. They believe that if you're competent to drive a car, you should be allowed to do it – in any kind of traffic. On the other hand, if you cause an accident, you're hit with a stiff fine to pay restitution to the injured party.'

'Pretty heavy,' Leif said.

'It's driving the regular politicians crazy – not to mention the insurance companies and the personal-injury lawyers,' the young woman said. 'But Derle has the money to blow a serious amount of zeroes on ads – and he's gathering in a lot of people who agree with him. For now he's concentrating his efforts on his home state to build up a grassroots effort.'

The publicist rolled her eyes. 'But you know what they say. As California goes, so goes the rest of the country – sooner or later.'

Leif frowned. He'd heard some of his wealthy pals spouting that 'too many rules' line. At the time, he'd just dismissed it as everyday rich-kid arrogance. But maybe they'd heard this gospel according to Derle.

'Well, it's nice to hear that we can have a car during our stay,' he said. 'But I'm afraid we have to mess up some of your schedule. We need a meeting with Mr Wallenstein.'

The publicist stared at them in surprise. 'Mr Wallenstein.' I'm sure you'll be able to talk to him during lunch—'

Now it was Leif's turn to shake his head. 'I don't think he'd like to have this conversation in front of the other competitors. No, we need a private meeting, behind closed doors in his office. We have evidence that one of the teams is trying to cheat. He may want to handle it discreetly.'

The world-famous arched gateway to Pinnacle Studios looked like something out of an old-fashioned movie –

either a gladiator epic or *The Three Musketeers*, Leif couldn't decide which. The publicist spoke to the gate guard, and a second later commandeered his phone to speak with Wallenstein's office. When they drove through the landmark gateway, they didn't turn off to join the studio tour. Instead, they zigzagged between what looked like private cottages and open-air sets to one of the office buildings that rose on the seventeen-acre dream factory.

They pulled into a tiny parking lot shaded by beautiful palm trees. As they came to a spot, Leif read a sign posted in front of them. *Reserved for D.Z. Antonov, Executive Producer.*

'I happen to know he's out of town today,' the publicist said before he could ask. 'And I want you people in to see Mr Wallenstein ASAP.'

They walked into the office building and got on an elevator. The publicist pushed a button for a high floor. When the elevator doors opened, she shepherded them through a reception area and through corridors full of offices.

So much for the magic of Hollywood, Leif thought, looking around. *I don't know what I expected from the nerve center of the holo-drama business, but this isn't it.*

Except for the posters for past theatrical hits, the setup didn't look all that different from the accounting department at his father's company.

Through the open doors, he saw people hunched over desks, reading scripts, sometimes dictating into hushmikes. A few people were examining holo-drawings of sets.

Then their group turned into a new corridor, and the carpet under their feet became much plusher.

They approached another reception area, smaller than the one by the elevator, but also considerably more elegant. A young man sat behind a state-of-the-art computer desk that would have looked at home on the bridge of the star cruiser *Constellation*.

When he saw the publicist and the boys, he raised a hand. 'He's on an international conference call, but he'll see you as soon as he finishes.'

The Net Force Explorers spent their waiting time examining the exhibits on display in glass cases set into the paneled walls. Bathed in indirect lighting were *Ultimate Frontier* relics like a model of the first edition of the *Constellation* from the original flatscreen series, various technical doodads and weapons as the series had evolved, and service and dress uniforms.

Leif smiled at the so called 'handicom' that the first cast members had used. Supposedly the fruit of a technology three hundred years in the future, it was bulkier and cruder than the wallet phone Leif presently carried in his back pocket.

From behind his console, Wallenstein's assistant cleared his throat. 'You can go in now.'

He stepped to a heavy door and opened it. Leif and his friends entered the inner sanctum.

Ultimate Frontier had obviously been very, very good to Milos Wallenstein. The producer sat behind a wooden desk only a little smaller than the car that had brought the boys to the studio. From the color of the wood and its uninterrupted grain, Leif figured it had to be an antique. The government had declared a moratorium on cutting down redwoods of that size a good twenty years ago.

'You have a complaint to make,' Wallenstein said abruptly.

'Call it a report,' Leif replied. 'One of the teams

involved in your Great Race – or someone connected with them – sneaked into a hotel room overlooking ours and put us under surveillance. The only explanation is that they were trying to steal information about our ship's design that could be used against us.'

The heavy, bearlike man scowled. 'That's a rather large – and fairly wild – allegation.'

'No, it's a fact. You can call Ms Ramirez, the assistant manager at Casa Beverly Hills. She and a hotel security man named Harris will tell you about the unauthorized person who was in a room with a view of our suite. That person got in by bribing a bellman named Oswald. Three of us saw the dish antenna used to pick up radio-frequency emanations from Mr Gray's laptop computer.'

Wallenstein buzzed his assistant and told him to call the hotel. His scowl deepened as he talked to Ms Ramirez.

'Are you making a direct accusation about anyone?' the producer asked after he cut the connection.

'I'll only point out that the room stank of cigarette smoke – from the kind of Turkish tobacco you find in the Balkans.'

'So you want to disqualify the team from the Carpathian Alliance before they even have the chance to compete.'

'Certainly not. The evidence isn't clear enough for that,' Leif said. 'We merely want you to make all the teams aware that someone's been spying, and to be alert to the possibility it could happen again.'

Wallenstein leaned back in his chair. 'I don't think I'd like the repercussions from that scenario.'

'There might be more serious repercussions if the C.A. team cheats its way to a chance to look over sensitive, embargoed technology,' David retorted angrily.

'*Ultimate Frontier* is broadcast all over the world –

including several countries which are not great friends of the U.S.A., and the Carpathian Alliance isn't the only country of that type represented among the competitors. There's a team from the New Arabian Republic, which has several ongoing disputes with Washington – and where the people smoke Turkish tobacco. We also have a South American team from the nation of Corteguay—'

'Corteguay?' David asked in disbelief. 'Who could have entered a design from there? The government controls all the computers in that country.'

'The entry came from La Fortaleza, Corteguay's military academy,' Wallenstein said. 'I don't necessarily like the government there – but *Ultimate Frontier* is something that has transcended borders, including theirs. And *that*, I think, is a good thing. I don't want to create an international incident out of what should be an entertaining broadcast. An announcement of the sort that you're requesting would undoubtedly do just that.'

'But what about the spying?' Leif demanded. 'If you don't tell the teams that the possibility exists, nobody will be prepared to deal with it!'

'I'm reminded of an old French legal motto,' Wallenstein said. '*Tout ce que le loi ne defend pas, est permis.* "The law permits everything it does not forbid." The rules of entry certainly didn't forbid trying to find out about competing ships. I don't intend to micro-manage this race.'

'That sounds like a very anarcho-libertarian viewpoint,' Leif said.

Wallenstein glared at him. 'As a matter of fact, I happen to support what Mr Derle is trying to do. Does that cause a problem for you, Mr—'

'Anderson,' Leif said. 'No, it's no problem – as long as we know where we stand.'

69

Silently, he thought, *So here we are. Thanks to the anarcho-libertarians, we'll enjoy a free car. But we won't get much backup in a race that can only get nastier.*

He sighed.

Looks like Derle giveth, and Derle taketh away.

Chapter Eight

'Well, *I* feel ever so much better now that we've gotten things straightened out,' Andy said bitterly as they left Wallenstein's office.

'What do we do now?' Matt asked.

'The tour has barely started,' Jane Givens said, taking his question at face value. 'You'd have no problem catching up.'

Matt gave her a look. 'I meant, what do we do about the spying – and cheating?'

'I think Jane has the right idea,' Leif said. 'We should join the tour. Jane, could you tell everybody we were delayed by a possible security breach in our room? I don't think, given the lack of support we got, that we want to advertise our meeting with Wallenstein. But maybe we can shake the trees a little, and see what falls out.'

David's dark, serious face looked doubtful. 'I don't know, Leif—'

'I *do* know what a snake pit this whole race will turn into if we start making outright accusations . . . and the studio refuses to back us up,' Leif cut in. 'You heard the big man back there. Everything that isn't strictly forbidden is allowed. Do you want *everybody* pushing the bad-sportsmanship envelope? We have to be subtle here.'

'I hate to say it, but I think Leif is right,' Jane's lips quirked unhappily. 'We'll have a war, not a race. And it's my job to make sure the race runs smoothly.' She shot a not-too-friendly glance at Leif. 'Although it's not my job to tell lies – in spite of what some people might think.'

Leif just raised his eyebrows. 'I always thought that was a job requirement in publicity and public relations.'

Jane laughed at that. 'Call it more of a professional hazard. I'll cover for you.'

David still didn't look very happy about the situation, so Leif took their team captain aside. 'We know we're going to get zip in the way of help from the powers that be around here. If we push this, *we* look like the trouble-makers – and get lots of grief between the studio and the other teams.'

'So?' David asked.

'We play along, so we don't have the studio on our backs, while we pursue the matter of cheating . . . privately.'

David still didn't look convinced.

'Look, David, I know you want to do the right thing. But in the situation where we find ourselves, knowledge is power. If we set off a hue and cry, the race becomes a free-for-all – every team will try to nail the competition, and the guys who started all this disappear into the crowd. But if we keep a low profile – and stay on the alert for any other nonsense – maybe we have a chance to catch those clowns.'

David's expression reminded Leif of the time his father had bitten into a peach that had gone bad. 'So it's a choice of the lesser of two evils, is that it?' he finally said. 'All right, we'll play it your way. But we'll keep a *really* watchful eye on what's going on. And if we see *anyone* getting up to anything suspicious, we come down on them – with both feet.'

Leif nodded. 'Can't argue with that. Come on, let's make nice with Jane. Then we catch up with our cast of suspects.'

'Lead on, Sherlock,' David said.

They caught up with the tour on one of the soundstages just as the group began filing onto bleacher seats to watch the lensing for a situation comedy. Jane made her fictitious explanation, and the Net Force Explorers joined the group.

Leif recognized the show as soon as he saw the sets. It was *Old Friends*, a remake of a show from flatscreen TV, picking up on the lives of the original characters decades later. The cast of elderly actors actually included a few who had been in the cast back in the nineties.

'My mom would flip out if she knew I was here,' David whispered as they sat down. 'This is one of her favorite shows.'

'It's going to be a bit rough around the edges today,' Jane whispered. 'The actress who plays Monica just broke her hip.'

The scene they were watching did go on longer than it had to, what with actors forgetting new lines and writers coming in to tinker with the script, covering for the missing actress.

'We're not usually this bad,' a white-haired star assured the audience during one of these breaks. 'We really are professional actors.'

Except for the holo-lenses capturing the scene from all directions, this probably wasn't all that different from the days when they filmed the original show for flatscreen, Leif suddenly realized. Audiences probably sat on bleachers just like these and laughed at the same silly jokes.

Why are we watching so many holo-dramas which are just rehashes of shows that appeared a few seasons, years, or decades ago? he wondered as the cast and crew started yet another take. *It doesn't say much for Hollywood – or for the resident geniuses like Milos Wallenstein.*

'I'm afraid we'll have to move on if we want to keep up with our schedule,' the studio guide announced as lensing broke up yet again.

'How nice to know that all Americans aren't late,' a deep, heavily accented voice came from the tour group.

Leif spotted the speaker – it was the most hulking of the three guys from the Carpathian Alliance team. Many in the crowd broke into laughter. Leif caught a scornful look from a coffee-skinned boy with hair cropped so short it almost seemed as if his head had been shaved.

That has all the looks of a military haircut, Leif thought. *Could that be one of the cadets from Corteguay?*

An intense-looking Asian boy nearby took up the teasing tone. 'You only had to cross three time zones to get here. My team has to deal with a seven-hour difference. For us, this feels like three o'clock in the morning. And we were on time.'

Leif shrugged. 'We had to talk with the hotel people. Something about unauthorized use of a room near ours.'

'I just bet that was it,' the Japanese boy scoffed.

'Hey, idioms and everything! You certainly speak English very well,' Leif complimented him.

He got a haughty look in return. 'Probably better than you speak Japanese,' the boy retorted.

Leif had grown up speaking both English and Swedish,

his father's native tongue. He was fluent in Norwegian, Danish, German, and Dutch as well. Thanks to his father's business travels he had a smattering of many more languages, both Western and Eastern European – plus some Malay, Chinese, and Japanese. He certainly had the vocabulary to tell the Japanese boy to go soak his head – or do a couple of ruder things – in the boy's own language and with a passable accent.

Instead, Leif just shrugged again. 'I thought that's why we invented translation software,' he replied.

The tour moved through several outdoor locations – a couple of blocks of an old-fashioned New York City, next to the false-front wooden buildings of a Western town.

Then they arrived at the high point of the tour, the promised behind-the-scenes look at the *Ultimate Frontier* set. Because the mob of contestants was so large, lensing was suspended during the visit. But the fans stood in silent fascination as the actors rehearsed a scene on the *Constellation*'s bridge set.

Although he was on the set, Lance Snowdon didn't have a part in this scene. He amused himself by walking among the kids, glad-handing them.

'I hope you don't mind having us come in to stare,' David said to the actor.

Snowdon looked as though he were fighting not to laugh out loud. 'Are you kidding?' he asked. 'We ought to thank you for the break. Milos usually has us jumping through hoops with his lensing schedules.' The rakish-looking actor shook his head. 'He may spout the anarcho-libertarian line when he's talking to people, but on the set, he's more like a dictator. What he says, goes.'

'He's really into politics?' Leif asked. 'I didn't know that.'

'A lot of people in the industry are into the gospel according to Derle,' Snowdon replied. 'They feel they've gotten burned by the traditional political parties, but I don't know if Wallenstein or any of the others are really ready to change the world. It may just turn out to be the flavor of the month – something hot and new that dies out before the next elections.'

'And you?' Leif asked.

'I'm an economic determinist,' Snowdon said.

Leif shook his head. 'That's another new one on me.'

'No, it's a very old philosophy.' The actor grinned. 'Just means I'm determined to earn my paycheck.'

He moved on, and soon enough the tourists were ushered out so the serious business of lensing could be resumed. They were herded over the rest of the lot, finally ending at the studio commissary for lunch. The publicity people decided to try to split up the teams, mixing groups of various contestants at large tables.

Leif drew a guy from the African team, one of the Danish kids, a Chinese girl, his English-speaking Japanese acquaintance, the loud-mouthed Corteguayan cadet, and a very surly-looking C.A. competitor. At least, without Mr Cetnik around, the guy didn't claim he couldn't eat in the presence of a polluting American.

Letting the others go first, Leif took the only empty seat at the table, next to the Japanese kid.

'What were you saying about the hotel management?' the boy abruptly demanded. 'Did you break into another room?'

Leif gave him his best lackadaisical American shrug. 'Not us, but somebody got into a room that was supposed to be empty. The assistant manager called it . . . a security breach.'

Okay, he thought, *the ball's in play. Let's see how the others respond.*

The Dane and the Chinese girl looked disapproving. Security breaches, apparently, were out of their experience.

Leif's announcement brought a hoot of laughter from the African boy – Daren Something-or-other, he'd introduced himself.

'Security breach!' he scoffed. 'Sounds like a very businesslike way to say that a thief visited.'

'Cowardly Americans!' the big guy from the C.A. sneered. 'They probably look under every bed at night, afraid of what they'll find.'

'Crime-ridden,' the buzz-cut Corteguayan agreed. 'We have no such problems in my country.'

Right, Leif thought. *In your country, all the crooks wear uniforms.* He gave another shrug, and turned his attention to his food. The tree had been shaken, and only nuts had fallen out. But at least no one could complain that there'd been no warning if more trouble came down the pike.

He corrected himself. *When* trouble came down the pike.

After lunch, the contestants were herded off to the other high point of the day – their first visit to the special-effects studios. Computer effects made up an important part of many *Ultimate Frontier* adventures – spaceships, planets, stations, cityscapes . . . and, of course, the occasional character like Soma. Stored images of the major characters allowed them to do stunts that would be too dangerous – or too expensive – to try in real life.

The place where all this magic was created, however, was almost depressingly humdrum. It was an elderly office building with cracks in its stucco walls and a roof that seemed to sag in the middle.

'Looks like this place just made it through the last quake,' Andy muttered. 'You'd think they'd treat their computers with a little more respect.'

'Oh, the computers are in the same building as Mr Wallenstein's office,' Jane said. 'This is just a temporary location to accommodate all the terminals needed for this episode.'

Leif looked dubiously at the old, rickety building. 'Who's in here usually then?' he asked.

Jane shrugged. 'Writers,' she replied.

Most of the contestants eagerly rushed through the doors, where a baldheaded man in a white shirt with the sleeves rolled up met them. 'I'm Hal Fosdyke, the effects coordinator for *Ultimate Frontier*,' he introduced himself. 'You'll get to know me – and Casa Falldown here – a lot better over the next few days.'

Leif looked around. Fosdyke's nickname for the office building was horribly on target. The inside, if possible, was even less pleasant than the exterior. Paint was peeling on the walls, and several of the office doors were hopelessly warped. To top it off, cables writhed like multicolored snakes along the hallways, through office doors, even up the stairs.

'I'm afraid this building was never hardwired, even for the studio's local-net system,' Fosdyke explained. 'So watch your step – you never know whose connection you'll be stepping on.'

He picked his way carefully over cable bundles to a half-opened door and pushed it open. 'Each team will have a setup like this.'

The small office was now crowded with a quartet of

computer-link chairs. 'This is where you'll, uh, drive your spaceships.' The effects man gave a quick grin at the dismay on the contestants' faces. 'Your virtual accommodations will be much nicer, I assure you, but you'll see them a little later. Right now, I think I know what you want to see.'

He led everyone down the hallway as the contestants tiptoed and stumbled around and over the cable bundles until they reached a large room dominated by a fairly beat-up holo-suite.

'My folks threw out one like that – about five years ago,' Matt muttered.

Fosdyke flicked a switch. The image was a little cloudy, but clear enough. In the depths of space, a collection of ships floated. It wasn't a fleet. Each ship in the long line of vessels was one of a kind. Leif grinned when he spotted the *Onrust* – fifth from the right.

Many of the ships were recognizable types – styles adopted by the various sentient species that regularly appeared on *Ultimate Frontier*. There was a Thurien sword-ship – better balanced than the imitation model that had crashed and burned in the racing trials. Leif also spotted the spindly elegance of an Arcturan star-scout and a streamlined Laragant quadship.

'This is the starting line,' Fosdyke announced with understandable pride. 'We've incorporated each of your designs into a deep-space setting. From this angle, you can't see the observation ships – or the *Constellation*, which, oddly enough, was selected to be the starter.'

The view suddenly shrank down to one of two much smaller structures that flanked the starting line. 'These are the space-buoys which will mark the course of the race. They're anchored in eight different systems, deep enough in each star's gravity well that you'll have to drop out of hyperspace and approach on sublight drive. Unless otherwise specified, each racer must pass within three thousand kilometers of the buoy to register – but then, you know all that.'

We certainly do, Leif thought. *As soon as we became actual competitors, the studio downloaded tons of data to us – rules, charts, additional technical information, all sorts of stuff. David's spent every spare moment plotting the courses to the optimum hyperspace insertion point from each star system.*

He sighed. Undoubtedly, all the other competitors had been doing exactly the same thing.

'Besides recording the progress of the race, we'll feature action from the bridge of each ship,' Fosdyke went on. 'Here are the character designs our staffers have developed for the teams.' The starting line reappeared again, to be replaced by images of their crews in the same locations.

'Now we know why they asked for holo-images of us,' Matt said.

The character-design people had outdone themselves, Leif had to admit. He and the other Net Force Explorers looked like themselves, except they were in Fleet Academy uniforms. He recognized the Danish kids he'd seen, stretched taller and idealized into Laragants. Thurien facelessness made the Carpathian Alliance team harder to recognize, except for the blond girl's figure and the size of their hulking teammate. But for every race that had human features, the special-effects people had invested serious effort to make the team members recognizable.

Of course, the Arcturans are human-sized bugs. We won't see much of that snotty Japanese kid – except for his personality. Leif thought.

Contestants pushed forward, oohing and aahing at the

appearance of their holo counterparts. Fosdyke let them admire themselves for a moment, then spoke up again. 'That leaves just one practical point to discuss,' he said. 'Creating holo-proj images of the race and all the ships will go on in the time we can spare from the filming schedule for the regular episodes of *Ultimate Frontier*. That means we'll be working through slack time – evening hours, mainly. And we'll be aiming for one-take recordings to keep Corporate off our backs.'

The bald man's face suddenly seemed to fill with authority, and Leif could see how Fosdyke had risen to his position, ramrodding the precise and technically demanding effects for the show. 'Captains, be careful of your ships,' Fosdyke warned. 'If you make a mistake, that's the way the race turns out. There'll be no do-overs unless you *all* crash and burn.'

The studio had laid out a pleasant dinner party, including cast members, but the contestants were pretty quiet for the most part – thoughtful, maybe, or maybe just plain worried.

The Net Force Explorers' team captain seemed remarkably calm, Leif thought.

'We've got our course,' David told his nervous team members. 'And I take it for granted that there'll be lots of jockeying to get far enough from each star's gravitation to drop into hyperspace. But the spots I plotted for our insertions are calibrated for *our* engines. The other ships have other capabilities. We aren't all going to be aiming for the exact same spots.'

'I hope not,' Andy said.

Leif just nodded. That scenario could get very messy, very fast.

He walked among the tables, responding good-naturedly to some joshing about turning up to eat on time.

If David's so confident, I guess I can just relax and enjoy myself, he thought. Right then, he spotted one of the younger cast members of *Ultimate Frontier,* Kyra Matthias. She played the daughter of the head physician on the *Constellation,* half-human, half-Laragant. In make-up, she was stunningly exotic. In reality, Leif was a little shocked to discover that she was much taller than he was – and much skinnier than she seemed in holoform.

'Let's just pass right over all those "how's the weather up there?" comments,' she said when Leif introduced himself.

'I promise, they'd never even occurred to me,' he said.

At least she had the grace to look a little embarrassed then. 'I'm sorry. Studio parties always put me in a bad mood. The commissary people go wild creating good food, and the actors can't eat any of it. We have to be able to fit into our costumes.'

'I can't believe that you have to worry about that,' Leif said. 'Although I've heard that some chunkified actors have had to appear in holoform until they slimmed down.'

'Maybe,' Kyra said. 'But with holo-programs – unlike veeyar – lensing actors is still faster to produce and more cost-effective than programming. It's okay for stunts, where the image appears just for a second or two. But the programming just gets too expensive when you need a superb performance sustained over time. And unless a studio's willing to spend the money to get the incredible level of detail required, well, the image may be perfect, but—' She hesitated for a second, groping for the way to explain. 'Have you ever seen a statue by a good, but not great, sculptor? The muscles may be where they're supposed to be, the face will have the right number of eyes and ears . . . but it's not quite *alive*. Bad holo performances can end up looking like people filtered through a computer.'

'Hal Fosdyke said they might use scenes of us racers in the production,' Leif objected.

Kyra laughed. 'And whatever they use, the special-effects people will probably redub and enhance like you wouldn't believe. You'll be amazed at what you look like when they're through with you.'

'Great,' he said. 'But you still haven't explained why can't you enjoy any of this fabulous food.'

'Changing the subject, are we?' Kyra laughed. 'I still have to fit into the costume. That never changes. Besides, in the days of flatfilm, they used to say that the camera put ten to twenty pounds on the actors.'

'They also used to say there were faces that the camera loved,' Leif said. 'But when you get an exact 3-D replica—'

'But you don't!' Kyra cut in. 'On a standard holo-suite, everything is a little larger than life. You'll see big vistas, alien cities with huge moons hanging in the background, mountain passes crawling with soldiers, a spaceship swooping past a planet bigger than your head. And when the focus pulls in for a close-up, the people are always larger than you are. It's some kind of psychological thing, I think. Drawing on the audience's memories of childhood to hold their attention.'

She grinned wryly. 'All I know is this. If you're going to lens something larger than life, it's better to start with something a little smaller than real life.' She patted her nearly anorexic stomach. 'At least in some ways.'

The blond girl from the Carpathian Alliance stepped by with a plate full of goodies.

'I feel sorry for her if they lens her team,' Kyra said. 'She may look gorgeous in person, but as a holo character she'll probably end up looking like a blimp.'

Chapter Nine

Milos Wallenstein arrived to make a brief speech at the dinner party. 'Don't go filling yourself up so much that you'll want a nap!' he warned. 'We'll be recording the first racing scene tonight.'

Leif knew this race wasn't going to be something like the Kentucky Derby, finished in two minutes. Or even like the Indianapolis 500, running over a weekend. Operating under the technology of *Ultimate Frontier*, traveling to a different star system – even a nearby one – meant a journey of several days.

The racecourse that Wallenstein and the *Ultimate Frontier* writers had come up with would take weeks to traverse if they were doing it in real-time, but there were only a few hours of 'exciting parts' that the show had to record. Hollywood rarely worried about the real laws of physics – so star-traveling vessels as they were presented in *Ultimate Frontier* used two kind of drives. The first was a sublight drive. This drive could only maneuver the ship at speeds below or approaching the speed of light. The drive warped the fabric of space, curving it ahead of the ship so that the vessel literally 'fell' downhill along the curve. Increasing the engine power steepened the curvature of space and made the ship fall faster. Decreasing the power reduced the curve and slowed the ship down. As the ship approached light-speed, its hyperdrive engines kicked in. These engines, once the ship reached a velocity sufficiently close to the speed of light, could stress the boundaries of space and time, already tenuous at that speed, and send the vessel into an alternate dimension, something called hyperspace. In the strange, fictional universe of hyperspace – a mass-less no-man's-land not subject to the laws of relativity, or to any laws at all but those the writers imposed – vessels could vastly exceed the speed of light by hooking onto flows of space/time called hyperspace currents.

On the show, these hyperspace segments were quite beautiful, which was undoubtedly a consideration when the universe of *Ultimate Frontier* was set up. The star cruiser *Constellation* would throw out umbrella-shaped force-fields to catch a current. The fields might look as delicate and shimmering as a soap bubble, but they were incredibly strong. Shifting the field like the sails of an old-fashioned windjammer, the star cruiser could race at many multiples of light-speed.

David had charts that showed the nearby hyperspace currents for each of the systems they had to visit. The tricky part for any captain was figuring out where to burst into hyperspace and catch his ride to the next star. Do it too soon, and you might undershoot your current and be stuck motionless in hyperspace; then you'd have to drop out and try it again from scratch. Wait too late, and the other racers would be cruising on ahead of you.

Once they were in a hyperspace current, according to the conventions established on the show, they'd all follow along the stream at the same speed. The question then became where did they break out into the normal universe to tag the space-buoys.

Again, timing was everything. Breaking out prematurely meant popping micro-hyperspace jumps to get closer to the intended target. But if the ship overshot its destination, the captain would have to search for a new hyperspace-current route to bring the vessel back to where it was supposed to go, or proceed to the target slowly using the sublight drive. Since the currents only flowed in one direction, it was impossible to ride the current that had gotten the ship there back to the intended target.

For the most part, the excitement of the race would come as the crews set up jumps from hyperspace, checked in with the space-buoys, then jumped back into the current. The crews wouldn't have to live – and *Ultimate Frontier* didn't have to record – every minute of the voyage.

Well, Leif thought, *I expect we'll be busy enough during the minutes they do record.* They had spent the time between the end of the tour and dinner checking out the Pinnacle Studios computer system. Each team had been given a corporate address. Leif smiled. *As if they expect us to get memos and inter-office mail.*

Somehow, he didn't expect a lot of electronic note-passing between the various contestants.

Or maybe I'm wrong, he thought, watching a couple at one of the empty tables. It was the pretty blond girl from the Carpathian Alliance team, sitting very close to the dark-skinned boy in the buzz cut who'd joined in the jeering at the late, decadent, crime-ridden American team.

The boy looked to be in a considerably better mood as the girl spoke with him. 'Ludmila,' he said in his careful English. 'That's a pretty name.'

He'd probably say the same thing even if her name were Griddalafunkadenka, Leif thought scornfully.

'Thank you, Jorge.' Pretty name or not, Ludmila had a

charming smile – and a pair of dimples that appeared when she used it.

They were rubbing shoulders as Leif got up to join his team. Ludmila glanced up, but her eyes seemed to go right through him as he passed.

What has old Jorge got that I haven't? Leif wondered as he made his way through the crowd. *Or maybe I just left my pocket Invisibility Shield on.*

'Ready?' David asked when he caught up with the others.

'As I'll ever be,' Leif assured them.

They headed out of the commissary and along the path that would take them to Casa Falldown. There was still plenty of time before that had to get ready for the race. But like several other teams, the Net Force Explorers wanted to get used to the compulink couches and any peculiarities that might exist in the Pinnacle computer system.

Leif's couch had worn upholstery – and its electronics were nowhere up to the standard of his personal link-chair back home. He gritted his teeth at the buzz that seemed to erupt behind his eyes as his implant circuitry tried to synch with the innards of the compulink couch.

They finally did, and in the blink of an eye Leif was in the system, sitting at a desk in a virtual office. It was a pretty bare-bones simulation, similar to what a lot of corporations offered to entry-level employees. The 'room' in which Leif sat looked like a slightly cleaned-up version of the writer's cubbyhole where the compulink couches were located. The desk was black-painted steel, the top some sort of recycled plastic. Leif could feel a slight slickness to the simulated wood grain under his fingers.

He always wondered why corporations couldn't dummy

up a nice teak executive-style desk in a fancy virtual setting. *Maybe the bosses don't want to give the workers ideas,* he thought. *Or maybe they're afraid the work force would spend the whole day in veeyar. I'll have to ask Dad.*

Leif looked down at his desktop, a name for 'work space' that had survived from the early days of personal computing. In personal systems, some people went to a lot of trouble souping up this area. Matt Hunter's desktop back home was a marble slab floating in space. Leif's own personal veeyar was an authentic Scandinavian stave house.

But in this veeyar office, Leif had only the fake wood top of his desk to work with, with three small glowing objects – icons – sitting on it waiting for him to call them up. The nearest icon was a small replica of the star cruiser Constellation suspended in what looked like crystal, except for a vibrant hint of electric-blue energy flickering within. Picking that up would launch him into the racing scenario. There was a small black icon, a stylized image of an old-fashioned telephone. That was direct inter-office communication. Pick it up, say the name of anyone in the company, and he'd be in holophone contact with them – or more likely, with their assistant. Possibly even their assistant's assistant.

Finally, there was an icon that looked like a note-sized envelope, which caught his attention with a winking reddish glow. That was his mail file, something Leif had never expected to use.

Maybe I really am getting company memos, he thought, reaching out to put his hand on the icon.

'List and categorize,' he ordered.

A sultry female voice – the trademark of a Pinnacle star of about five years ago – responded to his command.

'One message – category personal.'

He almost expected the sexy voice to call him 'baby'. Did Ludmila and Kyra have the voice of some old beefcake actor speaking out of their desktops?

Leif quashed the thought. 'Display message.'

He immediately recognized the letterhead on the page that materialized at eye level – his father's company.

The note read:

Leif,

I was stuck in a meeting, of course, when your note arrived, but I didn't want the day to end without responding. It seems that you're finding Hollywood an interesting place, at least. I'm not sure how to wish you good luck. Actors say, 'Break a leg,' which doesn't seem exactly appropriate for a race. Your mother and her ballet friends use a rather vulgar French word before performing. Again, not the best choice.

Perhaps I can rework something from one of my more colorful drivers. Smitty started out on the stock-car circuit in his youth. He always spoke of 'blowin' the doors off' the competition.

I'll try to go one further.

Blow their airlocks off, son.

Your loving father

Leif laughed even as he ordered the message deleted. He'd only sent the note to his father to test out the system. The last thing he expected was a mail response to this address. But he had to admit, the encouragement came at a good time.

All right, Leif, he told himself. *You're synched in, you've played with your desk, and even read the mail. Time to stop delaying and get down to it.*

He reached out to the crystal star cruiser, and the flicker of energy within suddenly turned into a lightning flash, blotting everything out.

When Leif opened his eyes, he was on the bridge of the Federation Interstellar Vessel *Onrust*. He was wearing the forest-green tunic of an Engineering cadet, and stood at his post by that control console. An automatic run-through of the displays showed that the racer was presently motionless, that all systems were on-line and functioning well, and that the engines were ready to go.

David turned around in his command chair. His tunic was gray with red piping, the sign of a Command cadet. 'Thought you might have encountered some technical difficulties,' he said.

Leif shook his head. 'Just stayed at the desktop to read some e-mail from my father. He hopes we blow the other guys' airlocks off.'

David's teeth showed a sudden grin. 'A little extreme, maybe – but I can go along with that.'

Turning to the viewscreen, Leif found the forward out-look on display, a vista of deep space with the *Constellation* off to one side.

Matt and Andy both sat hunched over their consoles, as if they could make time move faster by glaring at the starter ship.

They went through diagnostics of the ship's systems one more time, with special emphasis on the engines and the hull stabilization force-fields.

Then Matt got to show his stuff on the scanners. He focused on each of the competitors in turn: the lethal length of the Thurien sword-ship, the graceful Laragant vessel, the almost spindly-looking construction of the Arcturan fast scout. The Arcturan ship reminded Leif of a praying mantis equipped with engine pods.

'Speaking of blowing their airlocks off,' Andy muttered. 'I know we're supposed to be overpowered for our weight, but what stops that thing from tearing itself to pieces?'

'Inertia compensators and very little else. The ship's consistent with Arcturan building practices,' David said. 'Their capital vessels, the Queen ships, are heavily armored dreadnoughts. But the drone-piloted scout ships are more agile . . . and fragile.'

'Stepping from the mythical Co-Prosperity Sphere to the real Japan, it's the difference between the battleship *Yamato* and the Zero fighter in World War Two,' said Matt, who had an interest in military history.

'If you say so,' Leif said. At least Matt had shown he knew how to get and keep things in view.

Next it was Andy's turn. 'The right course is already input. Here it is.' He displayed their course as a dotted line receding into the distance on the viewscreen. 'It's pretty straightforward. Note – we go straight ahead. Maintain that line until we'd be just beyond the orbit of Uranus if this were the Solar System, a couple of billion miles. Then—' he pointed to a spot on the viewscreen representation of the course – 'right here, we go for hyperspace insertion, Leif brings up the sails, and we sit back and see how sweaty our uniforms get.'

'Fine,' David said, 'unless somebody tries to cut us off.'

'I've got all the standard evasion patterns we discussed already programmed for execution at an instant's notice,' Andy replied, a little exasperated. 'And I will be sitting right here at the console.'

'I think we're all getting a little nervous,' Leif said.

'Tell me about it,' Matt said. 'I think my antiperspirant is failing even as we speak.'

But there were still long minutes to wait until the race was to start, lots of time for all the crew members to fret.

Then the lights aboard the *Onrust* suddenly dimmed, and a loud voice came out of thin air. 'All right, racers, we go with the sim in two minutes, counting now. Count off, please, and let us know you're ready.'

The illumination returned to normal. 'I didn't know they could do that – ' Matt began, but he was shushed as voices announced the title of their vessels and the readiness to race.

Then it was David's turn. '*Onrust* – all systems ready.'

The muscles in Leif's stomach contracted as if this were an actual launch.

Please, he prayed silently, *don't let me be the one who blows us up this time.*

David ordered the ship's computer to go into the countdown. Everyone knew the equivalent of the starting gun. The *Constellation* would fire a non-warhead tracer torp high above the plane of space the racers occupied. When they saw that stuttering red flash, they'd be off!

Less than ten seconds now. Leif checked the crucial systems. Force-fields. Engines. Inertia compensators. It wouldn't help much if they took off like a bat out of you-know-where, only to have the acceleration smear them like peanut butter all over the rear wall of the bridge cabin.

They were ready. They were out of time.

'There it is!'

'Deploy!' David ordered with all the authority of a star-cruiser captain.

They were off without even a jerk. The inertia compensators were doing their job. Leif kept checking his systems. Everything in the green –

On the viewscreen, the Thurien sword-ship suddenly lurched into the lead, cutting across the courses of several other racers. The Arcturan scout tried to sheer off – a maneuver that didn't quite work out as planned.

An engine pod took itself out of harm's way faster than the rest of the scout. It just tore loose from the spindly sponsors on the insectlike craft and took off like the *Constellation*'s blazing signal rocket. The Arcturan's inertia compensators were clearly not doing their jobs.

And the Arcturan's engine pod was zooming right across the line of the race.

The floor bucked slightly under them as Andy evaded the navigation hazard. Leif checked his own ship's compensators.

Matt was handling the scanners like a pro. The viewscreen broke into separate facets, showing the way ahead, what was happening on either side, and a rearview shot as well.

As the *Onrust* dove below the line of the race, swooping down and then swinging back on course, the escaped engine struck one of the other racers broadside.

The ship had the blocky construction of the Reorganized Ank'tay Empire – *Ultimate Frontier*'s equivalent to China. But it was a racer – lightweight in comparison to most spacers. The engine pod struck it like a torpedo and went up, converting itself and the imperial ship into a cloud of plasma that grew and spread across the rearview screen.

'Anybody behind that will get fried,' Matt said in a shocked voice.

'Forget what's behind us,' David snapped. 'We're coming up on our hyperspace insertion point in four seconds . . . three . . .'

Energy levels rising, Leif thought. *Here we go . . .*

'Insertion!'

The view on the screens went from normal space to a weird, ghostly gray – the typical view of hyperspace.

Watching it on the holo, Leif was always reminded of a very thin fog. Except that, at various points in the indistinct vista, traces of phosphorescence could be detected.

Those were the hyperspace currents.

'Scanners show we're aligned with the current we want!' Matt reported.

'Deploy sails!' David ordered.

This was Leif's job. His hands darted over his console, activating the preprogrammed force-field array.

'Under way,' he announced.

Matt was busy fine-tuning the scanners to penetrate the hyperspace murk as best he could. Tiny sparks appeared on the display.

'I detect three ships ahead of us, riding the current,' he reported. Lights also appeared on the rearview screen. 'And lots more behind.'

Yeah, Leif said silently. *Just not as many as we'd expected.*

Chapter Ten

The lights aboard the *Onrust* dimmed again, and Hal Fosdyke's voice sounded from thin air. 'That's a wrap,' he said. 'We've got what we needed. Good work, everybody. All teams can now disengage.'

Andy Moore had an incredulous expression on his face as the lights went back to normal. 'I bet they got a lot more than they expected,' he said, glancing around at the others. 'This race certainly started with a bang, didn't it?'

Leif closed his eyes. When he opened them, he was back on the slightly musty upholstery of the cut-rate compulink couch.

David was already rising from his seat. 'That was hairy enough, without things going boom right beside us,' he said, rubbing a hand over his face.

'Not as bad as when we hit Mars,' Andy replied. But his hand went to his stomach. 'If they're going to keep feeding us big meals before we go in and do these scenes, though . . .'

The sound of an angry voice came slicing through the office door, which stood half-open to accommodate the bundle of cables that connected the compulink couches.

'—must redo the start!' the voice cried. 'It is impossible

for *Eagle Maru* to have failed that way!'

'I'm sorry, Mr Hara, but we have several minutes of holographic proof that your ship could and *did* fail in precisely that way,' Fosdyke's voice replied.

Leif slid the door open. The snotty Japanese boy stood in the hallway, confronting the special-effects chief. Hara, or whatever his name was, seemed to be suffering from something worse than a post-computer crash headache. His normally intense face was twisted with emotion, and his whole body was shaking as he argued with the man. 'I demand to see Mr Wallenstein! We will not stand for this insult!'

Looks like he's about ready to puff up and explode, Leif thought, staring at the furious young man. *I wonder how old you have to be before you can get a stroke?*

'You'll see Mr Wallenstein in the morning,' Fosdyke said. 'He already knows what happened – he was watching the rough imagery. Since he was the one who called for a wrap, I'd say he thinks he has something he can work with.'

The technical man turned away. 'Now, if you'll excuse me, Mr Hara . . .'

'You have not heard the end of this!' Hara shouted after him, his accent becoming more pronounced with every word he spoke. 'I will not let this go!'

He whipped around, glaring at Leif, who had witnessed his humiliation. Then Hara stomped down the hall in the opposite direction, muttering in Japanese.

Leif couldn't exactly hear what Hara was saying. But he did catch the word *gaijin*, an uncomplimentary term the Japanese used for foreigners – especially Caucasians.

Matt appeared at Leif's elbow. 'What's going on out there?'

'A lesson in international relations,' Leif replied. 'The Japanese market is complaining about the amount of air time they'll be enjoying in the episode.'

Behind them, Andy laughed. 'Right! Considering their representative spaceship will be on for maybe a minute or so before it explodes.'

David, however, shook his head. 'I know Arcturan scouts aren't the sturdiest vessels in the *Ultimate Frontier* universe. They're manned by drones, and the hive-worlds consider them expendable.'

'I sense a "but" coming up,' Leif said.

Caught, David grinned. '*But*,' he went on, 'scouts are expected to survive and come back with word of fresh worlds. This one was designed to last the entire race. I can't imagine it flying to pieces at the starting line.'

He frowned. 'I mean, it made it through the trials to win the right to race tonight. We saw those races when we were preparing for the final round. I know that ship successfully weathered worse than what they went through today. I just don't get it.'

'Maybe the ship takes after its crew in temperament. Things get a little exciting, and it's kaboom!' Andy laughed a bit at the image of a ship's temper tantrum.

They boys headed out into the hallway, which was now crowded with the members of other teams. The surge of adrenaline from the race had passed away now. Most of the young people were subdued, even silent, as they headed for the exit.

Leif hesitated for a second behind his friends. He frowned down at the compulink couches. 'After the way this race began, I don't think I find that very funny,' he muttered.

He made a mental note to check into the matter further.

Then, with a shrug, he stepped through the door and joined the crowd.

The next day was supposed to be taken up with a tour of the Los Angeles area, courtesy of the studio. There was an autobus standing outside the hotel, and all the contestants were herded aboard. Instead of checking out city hot spots, however, the bus lumbered through traffic over to Pinnacle Studios.

Andy glanced around, his eyes bright. 'Change of schedule,' he muttered. 'Something's up.'

This time, they didn't pass through the fancy gate. The bus pulled up at an entrance more suited for truck deliveries. Jane Givens climbed aboard and went through a roll call.

'What's going on?' Leif asked, but the publicist only shook her head.

They rolled off again, up to the building that housed the *Ultimate Frontier* offices. There they disembarked and followed Jane through a new set of corridors. They ended up in a large conference room.

Even so, it was a tight fit for the crowd of contestants. There weren't seats for everyone. Most of the teams stayed on their feet, clustered near the head of the conference table.

Milos Wallenstein walked in. 'I know that you didn't expect to be here this morning,' he said abruptly. There was little in the way of apology in his voice. 'But then, the scene we did last night didn't exactly go as planned either.'

Hara's voice ripped out of the crowd. 'My team was cheated! The Chinese representatives were cheated! So were the other three teams who lost their ships!'

Leif winced. He hadn't realized quite so many competitors had been eliminated at the start.

'Mr Hara,' Wallenstein began.

'I will not be soothed!' Hara's voice was shrill. 'Is there holo-projection gear in this room?'

Of course there is, Leif thought. *Nowadays, every conference room comes equipped with it.*

Wallenstein hesitated for a second. 'Yes,' he finally said.

Hara pushed up to the front row, facing the producer. He almost tore a datastrip from his shirt pocket. 'Put that in the system and order it to play,' he said.

Wallenstein didn't like taking commands from some kid. But he took the datastrip and inserted it into an inconspicuous slot at the head of the conference table. 'Play this file,' he said.

A holo-image appeared over the table. It showed deep space, a line of rakish craft . . . but it wasn't a replay of last night's race. The competitors were all spidery-thin, spindly vessels, graceful in the way a flying mosquito was graceful. In the midst was a familiar craft – the praying mantis with engine pods. What had Hara called it? *Eagle Maru?*

The ships took off in a corkscrewing swarm, each competitor jockeying for position.

Like rush hour in Tokyo, Leif thought.

'There!' Hara's voice cut in as, above them, the *Eagle Maru* suddenly veered right to avoid a smaller racer that had dropped right in front of it. 'That is the same maneuver as we attempted last night. Our ship survived it. Study the hull-stabilizing field and the inertia-compensator readings, and compare them with last night's.'

'Mr Hara.' Wallenstein had run out of patience.

But Hara wasn't finished. 'This is a copy of the qualifying

run for inclusion in the Great Race, held in Tokyo,' he shrilled. 'Check it in your own files – and then compare it to – to that travesty that took place last night. You also have recordings of the bridge consoles. My engineer tells me that the shearing force last night was *less* dangerous than the stresses our vessel experienced during the trials.'

'Then how do you explain the catastrophic failure—' Wallenstein began.

'There is no explanation,' Hara shouted, 'except for one – sabotage!'

Well, the cat's out of the bag now, Leif thought in the moment of stunned silence that followed the Japanese boy's accusation.

Then it seemed *everybody* in the room began yelling.

The Japanese team wasn't the only one showing its unhappiness. The four other teams who'd lost their chance because of the *Eagle Maru*'s breakdown had joined the protest.

Wallenstein listened for a moment of two, then said, 'Listen!'

It was a single word against a blast of sound, but he was the one who won. The angry team members shut up.

'Mistake, sabotage, horrible quirk of fate – whatever happened, happened. I may regret it, but we're going ahead. For the last hour or so, I've been in conference with our writers. The explosion makes a good plot twist. We've worked it into the storyline.'

A new storm of protests met this announcement, but for all the effect it had on Wallenstein, they might as well have yelled at the table. This was not the wishy-washy executive who'd caved at the complaints of the Carpathian Alliance's thug/chaperon. This was the man who ran the show, telling everyone how things would be.

What had Lance Snowdon called Wallenstein? Oh, yes, Leif remembered. A dictator around the set. Well, the description fit the man facing down a room full of very competitive, very upset racers. Not very anarcho-libertarian. Or maybe it was. *That* crowd seemed to be very down on rules.

And that was the mess Wallenstein was creating, as one of the competitors suddenly realized.

'Why aren't you punishing whoever made the accident happen?' a not-so-apple-cheeked Danish kid asked.

Wallenstein looked him right in the eye. 'The basis of this episode is a race between a variety of alien beings who don't necessarily get along very well. Given the differences in their cultures – and the prestige connected with winning – it might not be surprising that competitors might go to extremes.'

'You're saying it's all right to cheat?' The words exploded from somewhere in the back of the room.

Leif cringed slightly. The big man had just about said it was okay to lie, cheat, and steal – so long as it was in character for the alien race the team represented.

That's no help for us – the Galactic Federation is supposed to be idealistic and high-minded, Leif thought.

But for a raid-and-trade culture like the Setangis – or for the Thuriens – this was like declaring open season.

Apparently, Wallenstein decided there had been enough discussion. He turned and headed straight for the door.

'Something tells me we probably won't be going on that tour today,' Andy said.

Leif shook his head. His friend could find something to joke about in the unfunniest situations.

David wasn't laughing. 'He's just turned this race into a

demolition derby, with us as prime targets.'

Matt looked sick. 'Yeah. Think of how many episodes have been about the *Constellation* investigating or avenging the unpleasant ends of Federation Fleet types who got whacked doing the right thing.'

'Just because we're supposed to be the good guys doesn't mean we can't be tricky,' Andy pointed out. 'Lots of captains have outwitted powerful – and nasty – opponents.'

'Yeah,' Leif said. 'But it's a lot easier to do that when it's written into the script. Here. The plot will follow what the racers do. If the writers come up with a way for Captain Venn to trick whoever blows us up, it doesn't really help us very much with the race.'

'We're stuck with defense,' David said. 'We'll have to watch out for anything and everything.'

'Wasn't that what we were supposed to be doing before?' Andy asked.

Leif ignored him, turning to David. 'How likely is that Hara kid's claim that he was sabotaged? All the ship designs were in Pinnacle's computers.'

'Where they could be messed with,' David said grimly. 'Remember how our lights dimmed when Hal Fosdyke made his announcements?'

'That was just to get our attention,' Matt said.

David nodded. 'But what got my attention was that someone was affecting how the *Onrust* operated – from outside the bridge.'

'But to crack the studio's computers – I mean, a big corporation—' Matt began.

'Casa Beverly Hills belongs to a big corporation too, and someone apparently cracked *their* computer,' David pointed out.

Most likely the same someone, Leif thought. *Oh, this is going to be lots of fun.*

Although Wallenstein had finished talking, he sent around a bunch of publicity types who talked a lot. They busily did damage control, smoothed over what could be smoothed over, took abuse from those who wouldn't be smoothed, and in general got the company's way.

Everyone received a new address in the corporation's local-net, as part of a stab at greater security consciousness, and an offer of a free lunch at the commissary.

Great, Leif thought, rolling his eyes. *So my dad won't be able to get in touch with me. I'm sure a different computer address will really slow down this character who apparently cracks systems with ease. And between the stress and the glorified cafeteria food, I'll probably get heartburn.*

The other members of his team had wolfed down their lunches and rushed off to Casa Falldown, eager to recheck the *Onrust* and create whatever measures they could to protect their racer. Leif had felt that he wouldn't be much help in their effort, though he had promised to catch up with them later.

He ate slowly, without much interest, scanning the crowd in the commissary. So far, no beautiful young starlets had come over to ask for roles in whatever project he might be working on.

And when he'd seen anyone he recognized as a member of a competing team, he'd generally gotten a glowering response.

For a publicity ploy that was supposed to increase world understanding, Ultimate Frontier *has only managed to create a bunch of new enemies,* Leif thought. *We were already suspicious. But after what these kids learned this morning, I guess inter-team friendship is at an all-time low.*

He heard a low giggle come from behind him, and shifted in his chair.

Well, pardon me, Leif thought. *Maybe I was wrong.*

Ludmila, the blond girl from the Carpathian Alliance, sat close to Jorge, the boy cadet from Corteguay. 'It doesn't matter that you're ahead of us now. We will reach the buoy first,' Jorge boasted. 'My friend Miguelito, he has refined the ship-handling software so that we can time our breakout to the nanosecond. We can ride the current right to the gravity barrier.'

'But won't that be dangerous to try in this system?' Ludmila asked. 'There's a black hole beyond our target star. If you don't break out into normal space in time, you could overshoot – and be sucked in.'

Jorge put a proprietary arm around her shoulders. 'There is no chance,' he assured her, showing off strong, even teeth. 'Our software is that good.'

I guess he's good-looking – in a big, beefy way, Leif thought. *Somehow, I though she'd have better taste, though.*

The conversation must have shifted to more personal topics. Ludmila's dimples showed again as she leaned close to the young cadet, her voice low.

Leif didn't want to listen, but he caught the word 'pictures.' Ludmila said it with a sort of sexy purr.

Jorge suddenly shot back in his chair, his eyes glittering as he looked at her. 'Of you?' he said in a disbelieving voice. 'You wouldn't really send them?'

Ludmila's dimples showed again as she leaned close to the young cadet, whispering.

Leif couldn't hear her. He decided he should be glad about that.

'Yes, I would!' she said out loud. Her laugh was a sort of

naughty gurgle as she leaned forward again, whispering.

'That is something I would have to see,' Jorge said. He dug in his pockets, finding a scrap of paper and an automatic pencil. Scribbling away, he handed over the paper, looking expectant. 'You'll send it now?' he asked.

Coyly, she shook her head. 'Tonight,' she promised. 'Before the next racing segment.'

Leif couldn't stand any more of this. He pushed away from his table, his chair making a loud scraping noise on the floor.

Ludmila looked up from where she was giggling with Jorge. Her face seemed a little pinker than usual – whether it was from what she was whispering or the thought that Leif might have overhead, he couldn't say.

I don't know why I care, Leif thought as he circled well around the pair. *It's not as though I have any claim on her or anything*.

He headed out of the commissary, looking for the path that led to Casa Falldown.

Chapter Eleven

When Leif arrived at Casa Falldown, his fellow team members were lying motionless on their computer-link couches. It was a little creepy just watching them.

Leif sat on his couch, wincing at the lousy synch-in. A second later, he was sitting at his virtual desk. No messages – what a surprise!

He reached out and picked up the *Constellation* icon. A second later, he was aboard the *Onrust* – on an empty bridge.

Unless they'd suited up and were patching in virtual hull plates outside, there was no way the guys could be in this simulation.

Of course, they might have gone to visit someone else's simulation. Leif tried not to think where *that* would lead . . . or what would happen if they were caught.

Leif pulled the plug on the sim and opened his eyes back out on the computer-link couch. He had the beginning of a headache, but it didn't come from the maladjusted electronics. This was stress, pure and simple.

Jumping off the couch, Leif jammed a hand into his back pocket and brought out his wallet. He flipped aside his IDs and credit cards to reach the inset foilpack keypad. Unlike most wallets today, Leif's was made of real, live (or formerly alive) leather. At least, the outside was. Inside, there was a layer of polymer embedded with micro-circuitry. A stab of his finger switched those circuits to the 'phone' option.

Leif didn't need to look up David's phone number – his *personal* number, for the phone in his wallet. He knew it by heart, didn't even have to resort to the speed dial. A muted purr sounded in the room – the connection being made with the physical phone in David's wallet. The question was, would the connection also get through to its virtual counterpart?

Oh, it was a gamble – or rather, an exercise in applied probabilities. David was very good at programming – even adding oddball quirks to everyday items. If it could be done, he might have done it.

Leif held his wallet-phone to his ear. The ringing tone suddenly cut off. David's voice came over the connection. 'Hello?'

'Where *are* you?' Leif asked.

'Huh?' David's voice went from bafflement to embar-rassment. 'We're in my virtual office. Meant to leave a message for you, but we couldn't remember your new system address.'

Leif snorted in exasperation. 'How about just leaving me a note out in the real world?'

'Huh!' David said. 'We didn't think of that.'

A second later, Andy suddenly stirred on his couch. 'We'll go back in together,' he said. 'I'll guide you to David's workspace.'

'I can hardly wait to see that,' Leif muttered. He settled into his couch and once again went through the teeth-gritting process of synching in.

When he opened his eyes, he was in the same old office

– except Andy was there with him.

'Why are we in my office?' Leif asked.

'Actually, it's *my* office,' Andy told him. 'The minute I came in here, I drew an X on the wall.' He pointed to a huge scrawled X behind the desk.

'Talk about creepy,' Leif said. 'You mean all of Pinnacle's people get the same cruddy virtual space?'

'Oh, I think folks like Milos Wallenstein probably get something a little nicer,' Andy replied. 'And if you have a little programming ability, you can modify the space.'

He took a program icon out of his pocket. 'Wait till you see what David did.'

Grabbing Leif's hand, Andy activated the program. They went through a moment of darkness like an eye blink. A second later, they stood in what looked like a Hollywood designer's dream of a South Seas grass shack. Brilliant sunshine filtered through the woven roof and walls. From nearby came the pleasant roar of the surf and the calls of exotic birds.

'I love what you've done with the place,' Leif said with a smile. 'My father actually took us off for vacation to someplace like this once. The bugs drove us crazy.'

'No bugs here,' David said. 'I specifically programmed 'em out.' He sat cross-legged at a low table that served as his workspace. Unlike Leif's desktop, there were icons galore. Some Leif recognized; others made no sense at all to his eyes.

'I can see you've been busy,' he said, looking down at the small collection of items directly in front of David. They were even odder than usual – a small spool of thread, a tiny bottle, and what looked like an old wooden match stick – odds and ends at best, trash at worse. Except that they were on the desktop, and they glowed slightly. They represented programs David and the others had crafted. 'What do they do?' Leif asked. 'Vaporize any intruders?'

'We figure whoever is hacking into the systems is too good to be caught by virtual burglar alarms,' Matt said.

'They've got to be pretty good if they could get in, weaken the structure of the Arcturan ship, and fix it so that the engineering console was hoaxed,' David said. 'They could probably outclass any direct, active security measures we might program in to protect the ship – though we tried them anyway.' He pointed to a group of high-tech-looking doodads off to one side. 'That's the best and the brightest in the way of virtual security. Tamper with the *Onrust*, and they'll scream bloody murder. So far, at least, they seem to be working. I compared the ship against the original specs we turned over to Pinnacle. The *Onrust* appears to be untampered with.'

'We figure our friendly neighborhood hackers will expect to see top-flight security systems – and probably know how to beat them all,' Matt said.

Andy grinned. 'So we decided to go for indirect – and passive.'

'Rather than a burglar alarm that would contact us if something was up – and form a connection our techno-burglars could spot – we're trying simpler tricks.' David pointed to the spool. 'This is like a piece of thread stretched across a doorway – an intruder might not even feel it. But we'd know somebody had gone through.'

'The match-program is pretty much the same – like those old flatscreen detective movies. The private eye would tuck a match stick between the door frame and a closed door. If it fell to the floor – or was gone – when he returned, the guy'd know that someone had opened the door since he'd last shut it.'

'It's basically the same programming trick,' David said. 'Just a couple of lines of code that are erased if somebody goes into our programming, and another couple of lines that delete themselves if the ship's systems code is changed. The changes are small – hardly noticeable.'

'But we'd spot them.' Leif nodded. 'Nice.' He pointed at the bottle. 'And that?'

Andy's grin got wider. 'It's based on another poor man's burglary warning. In real life, you'd pour powder on a rug. If somebody stepped on it, the powder would stick to his shoe, either leaving a dark footprint in the powder, or a powdery footprint somewhere else.'

'I don't think it will actually do much good,' David said, with a glance at their irrepressible friend. 'But if anyone actually appears on board the *Onrust*, they'll leave a virtual "footprint." We'll pick up a new switch or two on the control panels if somebody breaks in. It won't be obvious to anybody but us – but we'll know immediately.'

'So what's left?' Leif asked.

'I have to install them,' David said. 'Give me a couple of minutes.' He gathered up the security icons, high-tech and low, in one hand. With the other hand, he went for the crystal *Constellation* icon. An instant later, he disappeared.

As he waited, Leif stepped onto the porch of the grass shack, enjoying the virtual sunshine. It was slanting in, indicating late afternoon. Leif was a little surprised. Did David's sim follow the clock here on the West Coast, or was it always late afternoon?

He glanced at his watch. It *was* later than he expected.

Leif thought for a minute, then looked at the other guys. He said, 'I'm going to pop out into the real world for a minute and use the phone.'

'Why not use David's?' Andy asked.

111

'Do you really want to leave a traceable link into our new, top-secret Net location? Be right back.' He blinked and returned to the miserable office in Casa Falldown. Reaching for the phone, he contacted central reception to find out what, if any, cab services Pinnacle Studios used. Next he called for a cab. Then he popped back into David's tropical paradise and told his friends what he'd done.

'I don't know if that bus is still waiting for us, but I'd like to get back to the hotel for a while – and eat something that isn't commissary food.' He grinned at the others. 'Since it's my problem, it's my treat.'

David reappeared, and they all disconnected from the world of veeyar.

'Did they say when that cab was arriving?' Matt asked as he got off his computer-link couch.

'Couple of minutes.' Leif was the last one out of the crowded little office space. As he left, he pulled the door as far as it would close against the bundle of cables snaking in to connect the couches. Then he slipped a tiny, intricately folded piece of paper into the crack between the door and the frame.

'What are you doing?' Andy asked.

'The same as we were doing in veeyar – only out here in the physical world,' Leif replied. 'If somebody tries to get in there, we'll know about it.'

His teammates were quiet as they filed out of Casa Falldown. There were too many unpleasant things a technically skilled person could do to computer-link equipment.

I think I made this a heck of a lot more real for them, Leif thought. *But we don't know how hard the other side is willing to play . . .*

★ ★ ★

When he arrived back at the hotel, the reception desk had a message for him. The clerk called it up on his display. 'A Mr Courcy tried to reach you,' he read.

Leif grinned. Alexis de Courcy was one of a handful of rich kids who tried to keep the memory of the Jet Set and the Euro-Brats alive in the world today. Leif sometimes played at being a playboy. Alex was one. And surprisingly, he was also a very nice guy. They had gotten together in Washington, Paris, Tokyo, and dozens of other world capitals and fun cities.

Could Alex be out here? Leif asked if there was a number.

There was, but the code told Leif that the number was in Washington.

The boys went upstairs, and Leif headed straight for the suite's computer-link couch. The equipment in the hotel was much better maintained than the stuff they were using at the studio. He passed smoothly into veeyar – in this case, a duplicate of the suite's living room – and went to the line of icons on the lamp table. There was a stylized lightning bolt among them. Leif picked it up, recited the number he'd gotten at the front desk, and in a moment was flying through the night sky over an incredible neon cityscape. Because he had the time and enjoyed the sensation, he took the scenic route.

He had visited Las Vegas in the real world, the home of bright lights and gaudy holo-displays. But the sheer size, scale and gaudiness of the Net made real-life Vegas look as quiet and drab as a funeral parlor. The virtual buildings of the Net were completely constructed of light: brighter, more complicated versions of the glowing force-fields of *Ultimate Frontier*. Leif flew past great blazing skyscrapers and towering castles that would have immediately crumbled into ruin if they were built of mere stone and mortar. Giant logos of proud corporations seared his eyes. Smaller companies maintained more modest domains here and there, a place to rest one's eyes. And all through the great black canyons between these towers of light, smaller glows flitted firefly-like on their separate ways. Program orders, packets of data, and fellow veeyar travelers like Leif, they all sought their destinations.

Leif flew onward across the Net until he too reached his target. It was a virtual replica of a fancy Washington hotel – larger and more dazzling than its real-life counterpart. Would he be deflected to virtual reception, or would this be a direct call?

He swooped to one of the windows in an upper floor, and found himself in a hotel suite that was similar to the one he'd just left – only this one was fancier.

The room was empty, but then he hadn't expected to be greeted by Alex himself unless his friend was already in veeyar. Enough time passed for a tone to have sounded in the actual room. Then Alex's voice resonated in the virtual copy. 'Yes?'

'Alex, it's Leif Anderson,' Leif replied, 'returning your call.'

A moment later, Alex appeared in the room and came over to shake Leif's hand.

'Good to see you, *mon ami*, even if it is your virtual self.' Alex gave Leif an amused look. 'I fly in from the Left Bank to find you've gone off to the Left Coast. Your mother told me about this virtual race out in Hollywood. Will you appear in the holo? The things some people will do to win even a small part! I remember Sylvie Lachance—'

'It started off innocently enough, and became a bit more exciting than I'd hoped for,' Leif said. He'd quickly learned that if you didn't interrupt Alex, he could talk forever – entertainingly, but it would go on for hours.

Instead, Leif explained how they had come to participate in the race, and the complications that had followed.

'Amazing,' Alex said. 'I don't know how you get into these situations, my friend. Your fellow racers sound very serious. They need to – what is that charming American phrase? Ah, yes – they need to get a life.'

'Well, everyone can't be as useless and charming as we are,' Leif said easily.

Alex laughed. 'Some of them seem very industrious. Using an old dish antenna to pick up radiation from a computer – quite clever.' He gave Leif an interested glance. 'Does your father's company still make those things? I bought one when you offered them for sale, and quite liked it, but lost it a couple of months ago. You'll like this, it's an amusing story.'

He listened to my story, Leif thought. *It's only polite that I listen to his.*

'We were flying from Munich to the Greek islands when we got caught in a storm. The weather can be frightful over those mountains. My plane was damaged, and the pilot said we had to land immediately. The nearest airport was in this awful, drab city. "This will be a boring stopover," I told myself. But I met this lovely girl, blond, dimples when she smiled.' Alex pointed to two spots on his cheeks.

'Oh, of course.' Leif rolled his eyes.

Alex laughed. 'No, it is not that kind of story. This *belle femme* showed me what little there was of entertainment in this backwater town – a pleasant enough time. I got on my plane the next morning , flew off – and discovered a brick in the case for the computer. Yes, the fair Ludmila was most certainly an expensive date.'

115

Leif's laughter stopped. 'What was the name of the town where you put down?'

Alex gave an expressive French shrug. 'One of those awful Balkan places. Somewhere in the *Alliance de les Carpathes*.'

That was what the French called the Carpathian Alliance. *It has to be a coincidence*, Leif told himself. Aloud, he asked, 'I don't suppose she posed for a holopic with you?'

'No,' Alex replied. 'I have a somewhat more quaint – or rather, old-fashioned – souvenir. A moment, please.'

He vanished, then reappeared a moment later. 'I had to scan this in. One of the clubs we visited had *un photographe* – a photographer – with a camera shooting instant flat-films.'

Alex handed over a thin sheet of plastic – the picture from the instant camera. It showed the sort of small table that expensive clubs all over the world use to jam more people into their seating areas. Alex sat on the left, one eyebrow raised in a slightly scornful grin at the photographer. On the right was Ludmila, the girl from the C.A. racing team, smiling, dimples and all.

Chapter Twelve

'What's the matter?' Alex asked. 'You look as though you've seen a ghost.'

'No, but you may have gone out with a spy,' Leif told his friend. 'This young woman is part of a team competing in the race – from the Carpathian Alliance. If they win, they stand at least to see, and possibly even cart off, some prime examples of new computer technology.' He looked at Alex. 'By the way, did you report your unauthorized technology transfer?'

Alex rolled his eyes. 'I was just asking if you could help replace the computer I lost!'

'Had stolen,' Leif corrected. He could see he was going to get nowhere with his fun-loving friend. So they talked for a while more, made plans to get together if Leif got free of Hollywood before Alex headed back to Paris, and then cut the connection.

Leaping from the computer-link couch, Leif went through the suite, rounding up his fellow Net Force Explorers. 'You're not going to believe this,' he told them. 'The friend who called in made a recent, unscheduled stop in the Carpathian Republic. And while he was there, he had his luggage lightened.' He went on, repeating Alex's story – and telling about the girl in the picture.

'You're sure it's the same girl?' Davis asked.

'Unless it's her twin or a clone,' Leif replied.

'She is kind of hard to miss,' Andy admitted. 'What did you say her name was? Ludmila?' He grinned and began talking like a holo announcer. 'Stay tuned! Our next program is *Ludmila Popova, Sexy Spy*!'

'Knock it off, Andy,' Leif said, a little annoyed.

'Well, we thought the C.A. team was involved in spying on us right from the get-go,' Matt declared. 'Now we know they had reason to be familiar with the kind of computer David was carrying.'

Leif just shrugged. 'The proof is a little late in coming. Maybe Wallenstein might have put his foot down in the beginning if we could have pointed to a single team up to no good. After the meeting this morning, *everybody* will be trying out their full collection of dirty tricks.'

'At least we know who we'd better stay away from,' Andy said.

Leif had to agree with that.

I wonder if I'll end up feeling sorry for old Hairless Jorge from Corteguay, he thought.

That evening, after a little rest and a decent meal, Leif and the other Net Force Explorers got in their rental car and drove over to Pinnacle Studios. The visitors' lot was a bit of a hike from Casa Falldown, but they walked the distance with lots of time to spare. Leif grinned to see the little scrap of paper still stuck in the door to their office. He and the other boys took their places on the computer-link couches and synched in.

Leif waited in his virtual office until David called him, giving the okay. 'Nothing disturbed that I could see,' his friend reported. 'I've checked all the telltales and run the file of the ship against our backup. Everything matches. I think we're okay.'

It only took Leif a moment to pick up the *Constellation* icon and appear on the bridge on the *Onrust*. Each of the crew members began checking their displays. Thanks to the magic of computers, several days of hyper-voyaging had been condensed into little more than an hour's sim time, the sim based on each racer's entrance into hyper-space and the placement of the force-field sails as they caught onto the hyperspace current.

Now the ships stood frozen in time at the beginning of the breakout envelope – the target zone where the ships would return to normal space, drive deeper into the star system, check in with the racing buoy, and depart for their next destination.

They all knew the hazards of this particular area. The current they were riding continued past the star and perilously close to a black hole on the far side of the system. Ships that held on in hyperspace too long could find themselves on a one-way voyage to oblivion.

'That Corteguayan cadet I saw hanging around Ludmila was shooting off his mouth about how well his buddy had fine-tuned the breakout programming,' Leif said. 'He claimed they could hang on to the last nanosecond.'

'Our own programming lets us slice the balcony – or the space/time continuum – mighty fine,' David assured him. He glanced at his watch. 'I guess we'll find out who has the best system pretty soon now.'

As if on cue, the lights dimmed and Hal Fosdyke's voice came on, checking that all crews were ready. As soon as the last racer reported in, the special-effects people began counting down.

The scene on the viewscreen abruptly came to life.

Four racers rode the current ahead of them – the Thurien sword-ship, a Vakerain scout, the Corteguayan vessel, and the converted Setangi raider. Behind them were the rest of the vessels still in the race, strung out along the current like the world's largest charm bracelet.

As Leif watched, some of those trailing vessels – the ones who didn't trust their programming or their engineers – lost the fairy flow of their force-field sails and then vanished, breaking out of hyperspace and back to the dull, everyday universe.

If they were trailing before, they'll be trailing farther now, Leif thought.

He rehearsed in his mind what would happen when the time came. First a few tiny changes to the alignment of the force-sails, to turn the ship slightly and throw it free of the hyperspace current they were riding. Then, sails down, and all possible energy drains minimized, leaving full power for the engines to drop out of hyperspace.

Each action sequence was already programmed, ready to happen quickly, one-two-three, when they hit the spot David had determined was optimal for breakout. They'd left the possibility of a manual override in place, in case something unexpected occurred, but the timing was so crucial it made more sense to leave the actual implementation up to the computer as long as things were going well. Hesitation or failure would mean disaster – they wouldn't be able to escape hyperspace in time, and would be flung along at near light speed into the maw of the black hole.

Sort of like the last spot along the river where you can park your canoe before the waterfall, Leif thought.

More of the vessels behind them winked out of hyperspace.

Maybe it's not a fear of their people or their machines, Leif thought. *Maybe they're playing it safe around the black hole. Maybe that kind of caution is why they're behind us, instead of ahead of us.*

Then it was down to five ships. David told Matt to kill the rearview, and to focus in on the ships they trailed.

The Thurien sword-ship looked like a beautiful but lethal weapon. The Setangi raider had the clean, aerodynamic lines of a ship built to cut through atmosphere. That was its purpose, to land on a planet and establish a trading connection – or to flash down with a swarm of its fellows and plunder.

Leif's eyes went to the Vakerain racer. It too had been adapted from a military vessel. On the show, the Vakerain were a contentious race living in a loose federation, member planets often squabbling and even fighting with one another. Their weapon of choice: their fighters – small, fast, and deadly ships that could operate for weeks at a time once separated from their carriers.

The Corteguayan cadets had chosen the best of the Vakerain long-distance fighters as the basis for their design. Leif had always thought the Vakerain ships graceful, but the Corteguayan racer seemed to have lost something when all the weapons pods were eliminated. Stripped down, it had hull lines that conveyed a sense of speed – and raw, brutal power. *Not a flying fish*, Leif thought, *but a flying fist.*

'We're almost there,' David announced, checking the readouts built into the arms of his chair. 'Ready, Leif?'

Leif snapped out of his musings and turned his attention to his own controls. 'Ready, Captain.'

A flicker showed on the screen ahead. 'The Thuriens have just let go,' Matt reported. Even as he spoke, the sword-ship blinked out of existence – at least in hyper-space.

'And then there were three,' Andy said.

'I thought the Setangi would drop out first,' Matt said. Setangi technology was not as advanced as that of other star-faring races. They made up for it through the skilled ship handling of their pilot-captains.

'Either their captain has lots of nerve – or nothing to lose,' David said.

With a deft twist of its force-field sails, the Setangi raider flung itself loose from the current. Then the sails collapsed and the raider was gone.

'Captain,' Andy was looking at his console. 'Aren't we cutting it awfully close?'

'I calculated this very carefully. Not quite yet,' David replied imperturbably.

They hurled through hyperspace, every second bringing them farther and farther ahead of the pack.

Of course, the Vakerain vessel was still ahead of them.

Leif began to feel uneasy.

It's like a game of chicken, he thought. *Who'll be the first to jump off?*

'David, we're almost out of the envelope,' Andy said, taking the words right out of Leif's mouth.

David sat watching the other racer and his instruments, his eyes narrowed. They'd reached the exact spot David had chosen for their re-entry. 'Now!' he said.

The computer initiated the sequences, one after another.

If any of these goes a little too slowly, we're stuck, Leif thought.

Trying to take his mind off that consideration, he stared at the viewscreen. The Vakerain vessel seemed to have cast off at the exact same moment as the *Onrust*.

At least, it was trying to.

Something seemed wrong with the fighter's force-field sails. Instead of snapping round smartly to throw the vessel free, the sails moved sluggishly. The ship was still being pulled along in the current.

'Kill the sails and get out of there!' David muttered.

But the sails remained caught in the current for a few fatal milliseconds.

'They're out of the envelope!' Matt cried. 'I don't think they're going to make it!'

The Onrust made its translation out of hyperspace. On the scanners, the ghostly fog of hyperspace was replaced with the midnight black of deep space, spangled with stars. There was no sign of the Vakerain ship.

'They didn't break out!' Andy said. 'Next stop, the black hole!'

David, however, didn't have any time to waste on their competitor. 'Matt, we were supposed to break out on top of where the race specs put the buoy. Where is it?'

'Scanning,' Matt said, applying a search pattern.

His voice sounded embarrassed as he reported. 'It's not where it's supposed to be, Captain.'

'What?' A lot of different emotions were squeezed into David's single word.

'It – it's moved.'

David slammed a hand down on the armrest of his chair. 'A trick setup! I should have thought of that. They told us where the buoy would be when the race started! But that black hole messed things up! The buoy drifted!'

Matt confirmed David's words. 'It's several million miles behind us – exactly where the Thuriens broke out.'

David turned to Andy. 'Plot me a course to take us past

123

the buoy and out of this system. I'll bet we'll still beat nearly everybody else.'

Most everybody – though it appears that caution had an unexpected bonus in this round. Leif thought. *But how far behind the Thuriens will we find ourselves? And how did the Thuriens anticipate that little trick with the buoy and the black hole?*

They swung around at maximum sublight maneuvering speed. Leif didn't even see the buoy as they flashed by. He was busy setting up the next insertion into hyperspace. They wouldn't be catching the hyperspace current out of here at the same angle as originally planned. Leif had to trim the sails into a new configuration to catch hold.

Something loomed in the viewscreen, then shot past.

One of the incoming vessels, Leif thought. *At least nearly everybody else is in the same situation as we are.*

They passed several other ships, reached the insertion point, and transitioned to hyperspace. Then it was a case of waiting for the lagging ships to tag the buoy and get out of the system.

Matt spent the time maxing out the scanners, trying to see who was ahead of them. 'We held our position. Most of the ships dropped out early because of the black hole, so they had even more space to cover than we did to get to the buoy. We've got four ships up in front of us,' he reported. 'The Thuriens, Setangi, Laragants, and Karbiges.'

That last was a real insult. The Karbiges were a race of living crystals. Their spaceships looked like pockmarked asteroids. At least the other leaders had cool vessels. But to be beaten out by a flying rock!

'We'll do better in the next system,' David promised. 'But this time we make sure we anticipate any hidden surprises. I want any possible drift of the buoys calculated when we set up our breakouts,' he added with a significant look at Andy and Matt.

Leif concentrated on his systems readings. *Glad it's not my fault,* he thought.

The lights flickered, and Hal Fosdyke's voice filled the room. 'That's a wrap. Thanks, everybody.'

Leif and the others cut their connections and found themselves back in their dingy little office space.

'I wonder what went wrong with the Vakerain ship?' David said. 'They were still in the envelope when they started breaking out, even if they were slicing it sort of fine. Why did they move so slowly?'

'We could ask them,' Andy said. 'They're only three doors down.'

'How do you know that?' Matt asked.

Andy shrugged. 'What can I say? I like to peek into half-open doors. I'm nosy.'

'Let's get out of here,' Leif said. He made sure he was last, tucking a scrap of paper into the door frame as he left.

Andy jerked a thumb at a door down the hallway. 'That's where the boy commandos were stuck, if you want to talk to them.'

That door opened just as he was pointing. A small, excitable-looking boy stepped out into the hall, looking back. He was lambasting somebody in pretty savage Spanish. The next person out was Jorge. The big, handsome boy looked as if he'd taken a hammer blow right between the eyes.

The smaller boy – the team's captain, from the way he was talking to Jorge – stomped over to the Net Force Explorers.

'Tell me!' he said abruptly. 'Is unauthorized computer communication allowed in this country?'

'Unauthorized?' Matt said.

The Corteguayan captain made a wordless, furious gesture. 'Announcements. Solicitations. Advertisements for obviously useless products and services.'

'Oh,' said Andy. 'You mean spam.'

'Spam' was the nickname given to electronic junk mail over thirty years ago. Just as catalogs, begging letters, and contest promotions had jammed real-world mailboxes back in those days, there were companies who targeted possible customers and converts with electronic mail lists. Spam was a definite nuisance –

Uh-oh, Leif thought.

'How could you allow this?' the Corteguayan boy demanded, horrified at the Americans' apparent acceptance of spam. 'Anyone using our networks for such trash would be punished.'

'A land without spam,' Andy said, almost dreamily.

Yeah, Leif thought. *A lot of things stop at the Corteguayan border. Like freedom. The government there doesn't want its people to know what the rest of the world is like.*

'Did you have some trouble with this, ah, unauthorized mail?' Leif asked.

'Trouble?' The Corteguayan captain quivered with rage. '*Trouble*?' You might say that. It appears that *zonzo* here gave away his supposedly private network address.' If looks could kill, poor Jorge would have been writhing on the floor. 'He began getting messages as we pulled out. Many, many messages. And Jorge, here, thinking that they were love letters from a pretty girl, just had to download them. Somehow, our computer's processing was affected. We could not pull free in time.'

'Ouch,' Andy muttered.

Leif ignored his friend's attempt at humor. 'Would it be

possible to see this mail traffic?' he asked.

The Corteguayan captain gave a dramatic shrug. 'Why not?' Give the gentleman your address, Jorge. After all, it is no secret now.'

Cringing, Jorge recited the address Pinnacle Studios had assigned to him.

I guess he hasn't done his military career too much good tonight, Leif thought.

Leif thanked the steaming captain and his hapless subordinate. He barely got a response. Gathering his crew around him, the Corteguayan leader stomped off down the hallway.

Andy watched them go, his eyes bright with repressed laughter.

'Spammed,' he muttered. 'He thinks they got spammed to death?'

Chapter Thirteen

Leif sat in the living room of the Net Force Explorers' suite, looking at the display on the room's computer. Using poor old Jorge's corporate Net address and the remote access code he'd been given, Leif was checking through the communications that the Corteguayan cadet had gotten while his ship was trying to break out of hyperspace.

His friends were still laughing at what they considered wild accusations. 'Come *on*, Leif,' Andy said. 'You don't really believe those Corteguayan rubes, do you? All the spam in the world couldn't have slowed the processing for their ship. These ships have memory to burn, and there are filters – I think the communications lines would have burned out before enough spam could have gotten into the system to do something like that.'

Even so, it seemed that Jorge had become incredibly popular in that short amount of time. There were literally hundreds of hits during the minutes the racing scene was being recorded. Press releases, announcements, introductory letters with files attached, and a few free-form harangues – all had been routed through the Net to Jorge's Pinnacle address during the crucial moments of the race.

Somewhere in this mess of tetrabytes, Leif was convinced,

somebody had hidden a batch of very nasty surprises. On his way to the mini-refrigerator to get a soda, Matt stopped beside Leif, peering in disbelief at the display.

'What *is* that stuff?' he demanded, pointing at a scrolling document. 'I've got a couple of years of Spanish, so I know that's not it. Unless the people in Corteguay use an entirely different alphabet.'

'You're right about the alphabet,' Leif said. 'It's Cyrillic, devised for use in Russian and other Slavic languages.'

Andy peered over, giving his friend a sidelong glance. 'Don't tell me you're reading that.'

Leif gave him a quick head-shake. 'Not much,' he admitted. 'But I can pick up a word or a phrase here or there. Like that. Freeze display.'

The computer immediately stopped the crawling letters on its display as Leif stepped forward to point. 'See these words? Savez Karpaty? That's the local version of Carpathian Alliance. As far as I can tell, these are position papers and press releases giving the C.A. position on world events.'

'Just what any young Corteguayan military cadet would want to receive,' David chuckled, glancing over at the frozen gobbledygook.

'It's what a Corteguayan cadet might get if he gave his computer address to a pretty girl from the Carpathian Alliance team,' Leif answered. 'I saw him do that, so how she got it's not much of a mystery. What baffles me is this.'

He gave more orders to the computer, and a new document appeared in the display:

A call to all free men and women!

Show your true spirit by joining the struggle! Protect your individuality by joining with those of like mind! Join together to exercise the power of the will through mass action!

The struggle is unremitting – the enemy ever resourceful. Yet the dynamic is never stable. The deniers of the soul may attempt to impose a status quo, but the triumph of the will is forever imminent. Revolution, like earthquake or flood, is always possible.

It lies within the power of every individual's soul to emulate the avatars of old, to dare . . . to do. Authorities attempt to monopolize power through a monopoly on rules. But the will to deny such trammeling of the human spirit, when conjoined with the energy of kindred spirits, becomes irresistible. The only danger then is false prophets, would-be avatars who seek to proclaim their own gospel.

This time David ordered the computer to stop the crawl. 'It seems to be in English,' he said, shaking his head. 'But it makes about as much sense as that stuff in Cyrillic.'

Leif ordered the computer to back up one menu. 'The source is listed as "The Wisdom of Al." '

'I can't tell you if Al is wise, but he's certainly out there.' Andy looked at Leif, his face a picture of confusion. 'What is this, some sort of wacko religion?'

'You'd think that from the language,' Leif conceded. 'But believe it or not, this is part of a political debate.'

Andy gave a great shout of laughter. 'Come on, Anderson, stop yanking my chain!'

But Leif seriously shook his head. 'AL isn't a person. It's the two letters, A and L – and they stand for anarcho-libertarianism. From what I've been able to dig up, the Net site where this came from belongs to a small group in Idaho. They've broken with Elrod Derle to form their own splinter faction – or maybe heresy.'

'I thought this "gospel according to Derle" stuff was for

public-relations purposes only,' Matt said. 'You know, to get people's attention.'

'Maybe it is, but this particular group has a definite religious bent – a sort of messiah complex.' Leif wiped the propaganda off the display, returning to the menu of mail items. 'Derle may have planted the tree of anarcho-libertarianism and watered it with a lot of money—'

'But it's producing its own crop of nuts,' Andy finished for him.

Leif nodded. 'People with all sorts of extremist views have found they can get together under the anarcho-libertarian umbrella. Derle himself wanted it to be grass-roots and free-form. That's how they've wound up with sixteen-year-old legal drivers – and a push to institute the death penalty for causing accidents. Right-wing types who feel that the people have abandoned their rock-ribbed principles and old-fashioned leftists who believe that the people have been diverted from their historic struggle can march together – along with nudists, people who want nuclear weapons legalized, fundamentalists of all stripes, and folks who fear that every race but theirs is being favored.'

He looked around at his friends. 'Does this begin to sound familiar?'

'A hodgepodge of ideology like that . . . sounds like the C.A.' Andy grinned. 'Or the S.K., as I guess they call it in their own country.'

'However, you spell it, the answer is the Carpathian Alliance,' Leif said grimly. 'Some of the more far-out fringes of Derle's make a religion of "going it alone." And what better real-world example can they find than the Carpathian Alliance?'

Matt's face twisted. 'Yeah, those guys *have* to go it alone.

They're a pariah state – international criminals. No self-respecting countries will have anything to do with them.'

'And they're being punished by sanctions and embargoes,' David added. 'Part of that "monopoly of rules" stuff.'

'Can these guys be serious?' Matt demanded.

'Who can tell?' Leif said honestly, continuing to scroll upward through entries. 'Serious or not, willing or unwitting, I think they helped sabotage the Corteguayan team.'

He suddenly paused. At the top of the listing was an address from the Carpathian Alliance – personal, not some government agency. It was a big file.

Those have to be Ludmila's pictures, Leif thought, his face going warm.

Andy must have caught something in his expression. 'What's that?' he asked.

'Nothing,' Leif replied a little too abruptly. 'Something Ludmila sent to Jorge.'

'Feelthy peectures?' Andy said, laughing. 'Let's see.'

'I don't – ' Leif was furious to find himself stumbling over his own words as he accessed the address and downloaded the file. He certainly didn't owe anything to Ludmila. In fact, the thought had passed through his head to store that file for himself. If Ludmila wasn't embarrassed to send stuff like that through the Net, why should it bother him?

But he was embarrassed. For her.

Matt gave a hoot as an image began to appear on the display – Ludmila, staring straight at them with a mischievous grin.

'C.A. computers must still be in the stone age,' David muttered. 'Look how long it's taking for the image to download.'

Leif almost laughed. Trust David to comment on the technical aspects of watching naughty Net pictures.

Ludmila's bare shoulders swam into focus.

'If she's wearing a bathing suit, there can't be very much of it,' Matt muttered.

Leif was about to blurt out the order canceling the download when something weird began happening on the hologram. It wasn't showing any more of Ludmila. Instead, a big virtual stain appeared across the display, a vile, toxic-looking, glowing green spill of something that seemed to eat away at the image.

'Virus!' David suddenly began snapping orders at the computer. It struggled to follow his commands, running more and more slowly.

Just as the Corteguayan team's program seemed to falter during the race, Leif thought. He could almost see the scenario. Right before the race, Jorge downloads what he thinks are racy pictures of Ludmila. He opens the file, which slowly reveals her face. Jorge saves the file to enjoy later, not realizing he's introduced a fatal virus into his team's system.

Scratch one competitor.

The computer began responding again, picking up speed as David shouted more commands, his face tight with annoyance. 'No good. It terminated and erased itself.'

'Can we download another copy?' Leif asked. 'It would be a good idea to have some evidence when we call in Net Force.' He glanced around at his fellow Explorers. 'I mean, we are going to tell them about this, aren't we?'

In the end, the other guys agreed with Leif, but they didn't get any evidence. When they tried to access that address for another copy, the size of the file had suddenly shrunk

133

to zero. That decided Leif on a voice-only call to Captain James Winters, the Explorers' liaison to Net Force. As he input the number, Leif expected only to leave a recording in the captain's office.

He was quite surprised when the phone call was picked up. 'Winters,' a gruff voice announced on the other end.

James Winters was *not* a glorified babysitter. He had been a combat Marine, leading troops during the last Balkans blowup. And then he had joined Net Force as a field operative.

After selling his superiors on the idea of the Net Force Explorers, he had shaped the organization with his combat-wise, hands-on style. When the kids had thought they could help out, they had gone out one hundred percent.

And Winters had backed them to the hilt – they were his people, as much as the Marines in his old combat team.

Even so, and what with the East Coast time being three hours later, it was a surprise to find the captain in his office.

'It's Leif Anderson, Captain. I'd expected to leave a message on your voice mail—'

'It's the burden of every organization to create paper-work,' Winter's disgusted voice told him, 'even though we've supposedly created a paperless society. Virtual paper. Updating computer files. There are only so many hours in the day, and for some of them, I like to try and get some business done.' His tone changed. Leif could almost hear the sound of Captain Winters shifting mental gears. 'How are you and the others enjoying Hollywood?'

'We've met a lot of people you'd find very interesting, one way or another,' Leif said. 'They believe there should be fewer rules and even less government.'

'I thought that's what we've been trying to accomplish

for the last thirty years!' Winters growled.

'I guess it hasn't happened fast enough for the anarcho-libertarians,' Leif replied.

'That bunch, eh?' Now the captain sounded grimly amused. 'Yeah, they're the coming thing in California nowadays. Especially in Hollywood.'

'I'm more interested in the ones in Idaho,' Leif said. 'They seem to be doing favors for the Carpathian Alliance.'

'Why anybody would want anything to do with that bunch of dog-droppings in human form, I have no idea,' Winters said. 'But there are some anarcho-libertarian factions who believe the C.A. embodies their ideal of "power by struggle." '

His voice was disgusted. 'Dupes, but useful ones for our Carpathian friends. It gives them potential agents in the midst of the country they consider their biggest enemy. Agents of influence in the media . . . and remember, California is still one of the major centers for technological innovation. I don't think they'd get very many volunteers to help blow up innocent people. But if there's something that's not too difficult to help a state that's going it alone . . .'

'I expect you're right, sir,' Leif said. He quickly outlined what was going on in the Great Race – and the potential prize for the winners.

'Espionage, hacking by foreign nationals into U.S. corporate systems, and sabotage,' Winters said, summing up his report. 'Or teenaged zeal, overly high spirits . . . and a girl fixing the wagon of a too-pushy Latin lover.' He sighed. 'I don't mean to minimize what you're telling me, just showing how Pinnacle Productions will present it when we ask to start looking into the matter.'

'You really think they'll try to stonewall you?' Leif said.

'Would your father's corporation welcome a government investigation?' Winters asked bluntly.

Leif didn't answer.

'Pinnacle is a big conglomerate, with a lot of pull. But I'll start the wheels turning.' Winter's voice lightened. 'The easiest way to deal with this would be for you to win this race and deny them any access to high technology at all.'

He laughed. 'Don't worry, I'm not going to wave the flag at you. We're all rooting for you, but just in case, I'll go rattle a few cages at State and Customs. Embargoes are supposed to be enforced.'

Then the captain hesitated for a second. 'Keep an eye out for any other interesting activity. But do me a favor. Don't stick your necks out.'

'Us?' Leif said in his most innocent voice.

'Yes, you. Listen, I was seventeen once, too. Long ago, it seems now. But I remember that charming illusion I had about being immortal. Lasted until my first firefight.'

When Winters grew concerned, he usually sounded his most ironic. 'I mean it, Leif. Don't put yourself in the line of fire. I'd like you guys to keep your illusions intact for a few more years.'

The next morning, Leif woke up to find the suite empty. He glanced at the clock and whistled silently. Had he overslept *that* much? The hotel's restaurant would already be closing up for breakfast!

He was under the shower, hoping the water would revive his tired brain, when he heard familiar voices through the bathroom door. The guys were back.

A fist banged on the door. 'Are you awake yet?' Andy called.

'No, I just decided to drown myself in my sleep,' Leif shouted back.

He finished, dressed, stepped out, and found his friends all sitting in the living room.

'You were up pretty late last night after you got off the phone with Captain Winters,' David said.

'It's a case of "know your enemy." ' Leif stifled a yawn. 'I was sampling anarcho-libertarian Net sites. It's amazing. Some of their points make sense. Others – looney tunes! Some of the nastier ideas show up in the slogans. The movement started by pushing the idea of being an individual – then came mass action and stuff about leadership – "the power of the will." I followed that through a bunch of subreferences to an old propaganda flatfilm made ninety years ago.'

'*The Triumph of the Will*.' Matt knew his history. 'A love poem to Hitler and the Nazis.'

'But all the references to struggle – those seem to be based on Marxist theory – socialism and communism.'

'I thought all those were supposed to be dead issues,' David said.

'Now it looks as if they've found new life under other names.' Leif frowned in distaste. 'But things get worse when you hit the mumbo-jumbo about "avatars".'

'What are they?' Andy wanted to know.

'As far as I can figure, they're supposedly great leaders who, through the power of the will, created mass action that either changed history or created history.' Leif shook his head. 'If it sounds weird, look at some of the people they chose! The twentieth-century collection includes Lenin, Mussolini, Hitler, Stalin, Qadaffi—'

David's face was stiff with disgust. 'Murderers' Row.'

'Most of the characters have places of respect in the

Carpathian Alliance,' Leif went on, 'although the racists don't quite like Qadaffi. Not Aryan enough for them,' he snorted.

'Do they have others?' Matt asked.

'They have all sorts of characters. A guy called Proudhon. Napoleon, of course. There's a lot of argument over Jefferson – most of them think he's too namby-pamby. Alexander Hamilton has a lot of fans, but so does the man who shot him, Aaron Burr – mainly because of his plan to steal Texas from Spain and set himself up as the ruler of the West.'

'You notice that a lot of these guys seem to have failed?' Andy asked. 'Not that I'm complaining about that.'

'It doesn't matter to the Carpathians – not as long as they fought for some of the ideals these crazies want to believe in,' Leif said. 'What interested me was one of the first avatars, a commander during the Thirty Years War back in the 1600s.'

'Protestants versus Catholics in the German states,' historian Matt immediately said.

'There was a man who was born Protestant, turned Catholic, and became a mercenary general for the Holy Roman Empire,' Leif said. 'Through purchase of governmental control, he was running a large chunk of what's now the Czech Republic, and he ran it strictly for war – sort of an early version of the totalitarian state. His dream was to create an empire from the Balkans to the Baltic Sea, but he ended up being assassinated. They guy was born under the name of Waldstein, but the Germans called him—'

'Wallenstein!' Matt shouted, a weird expression on his face. 'Albrecht von Wallenstein!'

Chapter Fourteen

Matt strode over to the suite's computer console. 'Nice catch, Leif. Did you find out whether it's a coincidence, or if our Wallenstein took the name?'

Leif hooked a thumb toward his bedroom. 'It appears he was born with it. I've got it all on the computer – it had gotten a little late to share it with you guys, unless you like a three A.M. reveille.'

'Let's see what it came up with. Maybe I can spot something you missed. Computer,' Matt addressed the suite's system. 'Wallenstein, Milos. Display files. Execute.'

'Executing,' the computer's silvery voice announced as its search engines rounded up the results of its Net search for print and Holo News references to Milos Wallenstein's life.

A large number of references appeared in the computer's display, floating in midair. The likeliest looked to be a long profile in one of the Hollywood trade newspapers. Matt called it up.

'I've already marked the relevant parts,' Leif said. As the long article swam into focus on the display, several sections took on a reddish glow.

'Born in a Bosnian refugee camp,' David read. 'Bosnian Croat mother, U.N. peacekeeper father. Naturalized U.S.

citizen. Well, you're right. It looks like the name is real.'

'What I wasn't able to find out is what kind of anarcho-libertarian he is – whether he belongs to one of the factions that supports the Carpathian Alliance,' Leif said, looking at his watch. 'Shouldn't we be assembling for that much-promised Los Angeles tour?'

'We thought maybe you wanted to skip it,' Andy said. 'If I'd done as much research as you did, I'd just want to sack out all morning.'

Leif rummaged around and got his sunglasses. 'Yeah, but there's some more research I want to try – with Ludmila the Man-Eating Spy.'

They just caught the tour bus before it pulled out. A couple of contestants made sour cracks about 'late Americans,' but the mood aboard the bus was not the best for joking. These were not the happy campers who had assembled for the tour two days ago. Too much suspicion and anger had built up over the last couple of days.

The reason for the Corteguayan team's crash-and-burn must have gotten out. The young cadets sat in a grim-faced group. Two seats away sat Ludmila the spy . . . alone.

'You know what they call girls like you in my country?' Jorge asked in a loud voice.

From her red face and tight lips, he and his teammates had been taking their disqualification out on her for some time.

Leif dropped into the seat beside the girl. 'What do they call them, Jorge?' he asked, responding to the other boy's taunt. 'Heroes of the revolution?'

The cadet's face turned a sort of brick-red, and he leapt to his feet. Three steps, and he was looming over Leif. 'You stupid American—'

'You don't need to be any particular nationality to be stupid, Jorge. It's more a case of circumstances. For instance, giving away the means to access to your computer system when people are afraid of sabotage—'

The bigger boy's hands closed into large, meaty fists.

Leif simply glanced at them. 'Another sign of stupidity might be swinging on someone who's carefully keeping his hands down. That would be looked on as assault, and could land you in jail – since I don't think you can hide behind diplomatic immunity. How would a little jail time look on your military record, Jorge?'

'You—' The beefy cadet looked ready to explode with rage.

'Yeah. I thought you could dish it out, but you wouldn't enjoy taking it,' Leif said. 'Still, I've enjoyed our little chat.'

He actually thought Jorge might take a swing. But the Corteguayan team captain suddenly spoke up.

'Jorge,' the smaller cadet said in a warning tone.

Sure, Leif thought. *If Jorge screws up, it probably goes down on his record, too.*

Big Jorge opened his fists as if he were dropping a hundred-pound barbell. 'No,' he said, 'she's done enough to me. You sit with her, smart American. You deserve her.'

He stomped back to his seat.

Leif smiled at the girl beside him. 'I'm Leif Anderson, by the way.'

'Ludmila,' she said. 'Ludmila Plavusa.'

This one is someone you wouldn't want to play poker against, Leif thought. Looking at her, he couldn't be sure if Ludmila had been affected in any way by the little scene that had just been played out. Leif couldn't tell if she was about to cry, or have a temper tantrum, or even if she was feeling much at all.

141

She sighed. 'I suppose I should thank you,' she said in a low voice. 'Everyone else was just pretending not to hear what those four were saying.'

Leif nodded. 'I guess we Americans are too dumb to be deaf.'

Ludmila shook her head. 'We are what we are. I can't blame Jorge for being angry with me – after all, I helped knock his team out of the race. But that was what my team needed.'

'And you always do what your team needs?' Leif asked.

'I read an interesting biography not too long ago,' Ludmila said.

Leif thought she was trying to change the subject, but he said nothing.

'It was about an Olympic skater from one of the old Communist countries – the place doesn't even exist anymore. After the country became democratic she was criticized because she went out publicly with the son of the supreme leader.' Ludmila looked at him. 'She explained that dating the boy was one of the things she had to do if she wanted to skate.'

'I think I see where this is going,' Leif said.

'I wonder if you do,' Ludmila said. 'You have computers built into your offices, your hotels, even your houses. Do you really know how hard it is to get your hands on a computer in my country?'

'I know it takes a long night of hitting the clubs,' Leif said mildly. 'You see, Alex de Courcy is a friend of mine. By the way, did the government let you keep his laptop?'

For a second, he thought he might have overplayed his hand. Ludmila looked ready to leap up and push past him. Her expression opened a little – into pure embarrassment. 'If you knew about that, why did you stop Jorge? The two

142

of you could have a fine time calling me names.'

Leif shrugged. 'Alex, as I'm sure you found out, is a nice guy – with a lot more money than sense. When he told me about you, it was as a joke on himself. He called his evening with you an unexpectedly expensive date.'

That actually surprised a laugh out of her. 'But I don't think he'd be happy to meet me again.'

'Oh, he might be. He enjoyed himself,' Leif said airily. 'But he'd probably spend the evening with one hand on his wallet.'

Ludmila abruptly sobered. 'I didn't do what I did for money. That computer is the reason I'm on the team. It helped me work on the engines—'

'So you designed that sword-ship?' Leif asked.

Ludmila shook her head. 'Zoltan – the big boy on our team – had overall charge. He's sort of like Jorge – large, and he likes to be in charge.'

I'll bet, Leif thought, wondering if Zoltan was aiming jealous glares his way. He couldn't tell without looking back. And if he looked back, that might tell Zoltan something.

'But when I ran the stress analysis for the various engine types—' Ludmila suddenly cut off her flow of words.

Just when you think you know the face of the enemy, Leif thought, *the enemy goes and shows you a human face. I expected to be flirting with a sexy spy. Instead, I'm talking to a would-be computer nerd who'd go to any lengths to get a computer to work on. Maybe there's something to this 'power of the will' stuff after all.*

Then he thought, *We've got a lot to learn about our friendly enemies in the Carpathian Alliance.*

'So you're the engineer on your ship?' he asked.

Ludmila nodded.

'Me, too – although I might as well have been the figure-head. I was just lucky to be chosen.'

'I wouldn't think you were lucky.' Somehow, Ludmila didn't make that sound like a compliment.

'What do you mean?'

The blond girl just shrugged. 'Just what I said. I don't think you were lucky, considering the captain they put over you. How can you stand being ordered around by – by a black one?'

Chapter Fifteen

Leif stared at the girl for a long, long time. He almost decided to get out of his seat and just leave her.

At last, when he thought he had his voice under control, he spoke.

'I think you should know,' Leif said in a low, flat voice, 'that David Gray has been a friend of mine for a couple of years. He's the one who designed the *Onrust*. Spacecraft are a sort of hobby of his. Without David, my team wouldn't even have a ship. We wouldn't even be a team. He recruited us for another project, and then we heard about the *Ultimate Frontier* contest. But basically, I'm the engineer on our ship because I'm David's friend – and because *he* invited me.'

That's enough, he decided, his spurt of anger dying as he saw the expression on Ludmila's face. She looked as if she'd just been slapped – hard.

'I – I was mistaken,' she said. 'I thought that – that Mr Gray had been put over you by some government faction – some sort of quota. But from what you said – and the way you said it – I see that I was wrong. I'm sorry.'

Abruptly, Leif remembered that racism was one of the supposedly dead ideologies that survived in the Carpathian Alliance. All her life, Ludmila had heard about how hominids might have appeared first in Africa, but then evolved elsewhere – especially, of course, among the Slavs.

'I didn't think everybody in the C.A. believed that masterrace stuff,' he said. If he had a lot to learn from Ludmila, she had a few things to learn from him as well.

'I – I didn't really think at all,' she finally admitted. 'It's what everyone says back home. The government . . . our teachers.'

'And do you think your people are the perfect race?'

She gave him a painful half-smile. 'I think they're remarkably . . . human. Good people. Bad people. Smart and foolish ones. You make me begin to wonder which group I fall into.'

'Sounds like your people are just like people everywhere,' Leif said. 'I've traveled around a bit, seen more of the world than most of my countrymen. Lord knows, you can find a lot of foolish people in this world – and in the U.S. Lots of them live in California. Just think of the fads and the fondness for silly things.'

He leaned closer to her. 'But one thing I've learned from seeing all those people is that it's not as easy as you think to classify them. The fact that a person is of a certain nationality – or race – doesn't automatically make him smart or stupid. The fact that a person comes from a certain country doesn't automatically make her evil.'

Leif leaned back, a little embarrassed. *That sounded remarkably like a speech*, he thought. *And I'm not even running for public office*.

'Ludmila,' he said, 'you've had a chance to see a little of America. Is it what you expected from the way your government described the country?'

'There are things that seem strange,' she admitted.

'I'll bet,' Leif said, thinking of some of the charges made

146

by the C.A. propaganda machine. 'Do we look like a nation of warmongers run by a secret police?'

Ludmila seemed strangely wary. 'But – aren't you connected with the secret police? The Net Force?'

Score one for Carpathian intelligence, Leif thought. He and his friends hadn't advertised the fact that they were Net Force Explorers. But Ludmila obviously knew about the connection.

Did the mysterious Mr Cetnik have dossiers on him and his friends? On all the teams?

'The Net Force Explorers are a youth group sponsored by Net Force,' Leif said quietly. 'But we aren't cops. We have some training to help in case of emergencies, but if we saw a crime, we'd just report it like any citizen ought to.'

I hope that doesn't sound as stuffy as I think it does, he thought.

'But more importantly, Net Force is hardly a secret police. They're right out there, trying to stop criminals and shady business types from robbing and pillaging on the Net, not to mention protecting our computers from terrorists and—'

He paused for a second.

Ludmila looked at him with a laugh in her eyes. 'And unfriendly governments, no?'

'Yes,' he admitted. 'But it's hardly secret. I could take you into the offices—'

He stopped as a slight shudder went through her. 'The National Defense Police have offices, too – right in the middle of the capital, near Mesarovic Square. Many people go in there.'

Her voice lowered until it was little more than a whisper. 'Few come out.'

★ ★ ★

The tour guide tried hard, but she had a very tough audience. None of the racers was in a much better mood by dinnertime at a very trendy – and touristy – Thai/ Mexican place.

Leif was in a bad mood, too. The Carpathian Alliance team had all but grabbed Ludmila as they got off the bus at the restaurant. Once inside, they sat down at a small table, big Zoltan glaring at Leif.

Now that her cover's been blown, he's feeling proprietary, Leif thought.

To top it off, Leif caught that fish-oil taste of mock-meat in his burrito.

The bus ride out to Pinnacle Studios was quiet – *too* quiet, Leif thought. It was a sullen silence, from people angry at one another – and frankly worried over the next stage of the race.

'Would've been better if they'd skipped dinner and just let us go back to the hotel and relax.' Even Andy's wise-guy cheerfulness had taken a brooding turn.

'Yeah, and if transmat beamers were real instead of just special effects on *Ultimate Frontier*, we could have gone home and taken a nice nap,' David replied. 'But they aren't, and we can't, so we won't. Make the best of it.'

Leif and the others went to the writers' cubbyhole in Casa Falldown and synched in. He wanted to swear at that stupid computer-link chair, but that wasn't what was eating him.

It was Ludmila. From the way she had handled Alex and Jorge – probably Zoltan – she'd seemed like an almost Machiavellian intriguer. But after he'd talked to her for a while, she'd seemed like a shy little girl who'd never been out in the world. Which was the real person?

Was she both? Was she neither?

She'd seemed to enjoy talking with him on the bus – once they got over the initial shocks. Her stories of life in the Carpathian Alliance had been innocent enough – not a nightmare of oppression, but a land where people walked softly and kept their mouths shut. Her voice had taken on a slight ironic lilt when she spoke of the *domovina*, the homeland – a word C.A. propagandists must have done to death.

No, Ludmila Plavusa was no Olga Popova, lady spy. She was nicer than Leif had expected – and more puzzling.

He pushed the whole line of thought aside. *Worry about it later*, he told himself. *For now, you've got a spaceship to drive.*

The *Onrust*'s next destination was a bit more straightforward – no black holes, no subtle gravity tricks. The space-buoy should be where it had been left.

But to get to it, the racers would have to navigate their way through a big asteroid field.

In the old days of the *Ultimate Frontier* series, such a scene would have meant threading the needle between clumps of styrofoam rocks that seemed about twenty feet away from one another. But with people actually heading out past Mars to prospect the Solar System's asteroid fields, a touch of reality had crept in.

When you break up a planet – or proto-planet – and spread its mass across a half-a-billion-mile-wide ellipse, you end up with the pieces stretched mighty thin – miles, dozens of miles, even hundred of miles apart. Passing through all that orbital debris wasn't a case of having to watch for a new rock every couple of feet or so. It was a case of throttling down the speed to give your ship more maneuvering room. What you *didn't* want to do was hit a chunk of something while moving at a significant percentage of light-speed.

David and Andy had calculated a breakout point well away from the outer edges of the huge debris belt. They planned on making up any lost time once they were past the belt.

'The rock field only extends along the system's orbital plane,' Leif had argued. 'Why not go up and over it?'

'That's the dirty little trick they played on us,' David said, displaying the system in holo. 'The buoy is hidden among the asteroids. You can only pick up the signal when you are within a thousand kilometers of the buoy. You have to be in the asteroid belt to be close enough to have any chance at all of picking up that signal. We have to go through the maze to find it, and in this round of the race, you have to get within five hundred kilometers of the buoy to tag it.'

'With all the related thrills and spills.' Andy sighed theatrically. 'Can't you just imagine holo audiences all over the world, sitting on the edge of their seats, fearing – hoping – one of us will crash?'

'No,' Leif said honestly. 'But I can imagine Milos Wallenstein doing it.'

The bridge lights dimmed, Hal Fosdyke polled the crews to make sure they were ready . . . and then they were rolling.

They made their breakout from the hyper-dimensions to normal space without a hitch. David ordered, 'Commence braking.'

'Braking,' Leif confirmed.

He changed the warp of space in the sublight drive to slow them down from the headlong speed they'd used to get out of the last system. Even as he did so, another racer materialized from hyperspace, flashed ahead – and almost collided with something.

The racer sheered off at the last minute, dumped acceleration, but wound up moving almost perpendicularly away from the asteroid belt that hid the buoy.

'It will take them a while to come around again,' Andy muttered.

They continued on their course – a slow, almost glacial, progress through the asteroid belt – boring, really, except for the need for constant watchfulness. Matt sat hunched over the scanner controls, trying every trick he knew to spot debris. His voice grew tight, and he snapped rather than reported his observations.

About halfway through, Matt became even more active at his console. 'I'm picking up signs of a major release of energy,' he said. 'Looks like someone hit a rock.'

The good thing is, it gets us back concentrating just as our attention began to flag, Leif thought. *The bad thing is that there's one less racer. Although they were ahead of us. Does that make two good things?*

Just before reaching the buoy, they were forced to divert from their course. They had no choice – the route they'd intended to take was filled with an expanding cloud of white-hot plasma.

'Almost there – they must have gotten too eager,' Andy said.

'Let's not allow the same thing to happen to us,' David said.

'I'm scanning,' Matt said – almost a protest.

A moment or two later, they were in range of the buoy and registered.

'Now all we have to do is worry about getting out in one piece,' David said in satisfaction. 'Prepare for maneuver.'

'Helm ready,' Andy reported crisply. 'New course laid in.'

'Engines ready,' Leif said.

'Scanning?'

Matt's hands danced over his console. 'We're clear.'

'Deploy.'

Leif activated the program that manipulated the *Onrust*'s drive fields. The slowly moving ship suddenly changed its axis, tilting up almost perpendicular to its former course.

'Scanning?'

'Clear field ahead.'

'Propulsion – deploy.'

'Deploying.' Leif cut in the standard drive configuration again, sending the *Onrust* out through the 'top' of the asteroid belt rather than going all the way through to the inner side.

David was hoping they'd recapture some lost ground with the maneuver. Leif wasn't sure, but he had no time to think. He and Andy were too busy manually fine-tuning their course in response to Matt's shouted warnings.

'I think we're out!' Matt's voice had a sort of exhausted gladness as he made the announcement.

'Keep a sharp eye for any surprises,' David warned. After a moment, he ordered, 'Increase speed fifty per cent.'

'Fifty per cent,' Leif confirmed.

'On course,' Andy reported.

They keep accelerating until they were just above maxing out. The insertion point they wanted was high above the orbital plane of this system – where a very favorable hyperspace current headed to their next destination.

Matt finally shifted from short-range scanning for chunks of dwarf real estate to a longer view that showed other competitors. 'Thuriens and Laragants ahead of us,' he reported. 'The Karbiges decided to go through the belt before shifting course. They're slightly behind us.'

He continued to consult the finer readings on his console. 'No sign of the Setangis.'

'Too bad,' David said. He'd gotten friendly with the members of the African team racing as the Setangis. From what he saw, they were a scrappy bunch, who'd had to beg and borrow – but not steal – computer time to complete their design. Like the fictional Setangi, they had no technological edge, but kept up with a combination of daring and piloting virtuosity.

Well, either too much of one or too little of the other wound up getting them nailed by a rock, Leif thought. *I hope you're happy, Milos Wallenstein.*

They hit the insertion point and snapped into hyperspace solidly in third place. And while waiting for the longer tail of pursuing racers, they had enough time for Leif to try a few experiments at tweaking their force-sails to take maximum advantage of the current.

The lights flickered, but Hal Fosdyke's voice didn't sound for a couple of minutes. Then he finally said, 'That's a wrap.'

Andy glanced around, one eyebrow raised. 'He didn't thank us,' he said. 'Hal always thanked us before.'

'Quit clowning,' Matt said grumpily. 'I want to get out of here, back to the hotel, and into a shower.'

Andy grabbed the front of his damp tunic, whiffling it back and forth as if he were fanning himself. 'Good thing this is only virtual sweat. Otherwise the smell in that little office would knock you over.'

The boys cut their connections and found themselves back in Casa Falldown. Andy sniffed the air. 'Come to think of it, we could all do with showers anyway,' he said.

They stepped out in the hallway to find the African team passing. David stepped forward. 'I'm really sorry—'

The tall, thin, usually smiling boy who served as the engineer whirled around. '*You're* really sorry?' he began.

But his captain reached round, laying a restraining hand on his arm. 'Later, Daren,' the other boy said.

Daren's habitual good humor seemed to have deserted him with whatever catastrophe had hit their ship. He shook off his captain's arm with a snarl. But he did nod. 'Later,' he said.

The Net Force Explorers trailed behind as the African boys left the building. Leif noticed that they didn't head for the bus. They took the path that led to the office building housing the *Ultimate Frontier* production staff.

When the bus headed back to the hotel without the African team, Leif began to get actively curious.

'Where is their room?' he asked David, who'd visited with the team to listen to the music of the new African bands.

'They're on our floor, but on the east wing. Their room overlooks the pool,' David replied. He was still running a towel over his hair.

'What do you say we take a stroll over there? Either we can go visit, or we might catch them in the hallways.'

Just as they got over to the east wing, the elevator doors opened, and the African team members exited.

'Hey, Daren,' David called out, stepping up to the tall boy.

Before he reached him, another figure came out – a very flustered, harassed-looking Jane Givens. 'Sorry, guys,' she said, 'we can't talk. There's a personal emergency back home. These boys will be flying out tonight.'

'Emergency?' David echoed. 'What's wrong?'

'We don't have time,' Jane insisted. 'We're trying to catch a flight. Go back to your room.'

She herded the Setangi team members along like a mother hen. Over her head, however, Daren looked back and mouthed a single word. 'Outside.'

David and Leif shared one glance, then jumped to catch the elevator.

The hotel's inner courtyard was spacious and airy. But the desert chill was in the air. No one was swimming in the pool when they arrived.

'What now?' David asked as they stood among deserted deck chairs.

'Something weird is going on,' Leif said. 'Personal emergency, my pale white . . . foot. Jane isn't letting that team talk to anyone.' He stared up, counting the floors along the eastern wing. 'Which would be their room?'

As if in answer, a tall, dark figure appeared on one of the third-floor balconies – Daren.

'We wouldn't want to leave these.' They could hear his voice clearly as he glanced down at them. Then he turned, holding up a handful of swimming trunks that had been left out to dry.

With his other hand, he pitched a small white ball off the balcony. It seemed to come down in slow motion, floating on an idle breeze.

Leif grimaced. *If that winds up in the swimming pool –*

David made a jumping catch, banging into one of the deck chairs. Then he and Leif ducked quickly into the shadows under the lowest balcony.

That was a lucky move. A moment later, they heard Jane Given's voice. 'I thought I heard something out here.'

Keeping to the shadows as much as possible, Leif and

David made their way back to the hotel door. They headed round to the opposite wing before they took an elevator.

When the doors closed, Leif nearly tackled his friend. 'Okay. What did Daren throw?'

David held up a crumpled ball of notepaper. Eagerly, they straightened it out.

There were just a few hastily scribbled words.

Thuriens built weapons into their design – used them on us. Beware!

Chapter Sixteen

Leif and David sat in their suite's living room, letting the other Net Force Explorers read Daren's note.

'How could they have smuggled weapons aboard their ship? The specs absolutely forbid them,' Andy said.

'I can see ways that seemingly innocent components might be combined to create a weapon,' David said. He looked as if something he'd eaten was now seriously disagreeing with him. 'Something on the order of a laser, perhaps. Nothing like the heavy pulsers and cee-plus torps warships use in the series.'

'Against something as flimsy as most of these racers, a laser is all they need,' Matt said. 'Mess with one of the engines, and all you've got is a cloud of plasma.'

'More to the point, can we rejigger some of our components to pull the same trick?' Andy wanted to know.

David shook his head. 'This is a racing ship, not a flying warehouse. We just don't have the spare parts to do anything like that. I'd have had to design the capability in from the ground up.'

'And since all designs were locked in when we handed over our datascrips, there's no chance of changing that now,' Leif said heavily.

'Well, I intend to change *something*,' Matt growled.

'Starting with the attitude of the people at the studio. What do you say we march back into Wallenstein's office tomorrow and call him on this?'

'I'd say we'd be bundled out of this hotel and be gone by afternoon,' Leif said. 'Another round of "personal emergencies." The studio does not want word of this getting out. They probably didn't catch the weapons of the Thurien ship when the design was submitted. But now Wallenstein's "everything not forbidden is permitted" policy has turned around and bitten him on the tail.'

Andy gave him an ironic smile. 'Besides, secret weapons make for a great plot twist. Think how Captain Venn and Commander Dominic would end up handling them.'

Matt hadn't given up yet. 'We could go down to breakfast tomorrow and show everyone this note. If all the teams pull together—'

'I wish it were that simple,' Leif said, cutting his friend off. 'But it's not likely to happen. For one thing, everyone is so suspicious and paranoid that they're not likely to believe us. We're number three in the race right now. If we eliminate the front-runner, we become number two. So we have a motive for smearing the C.A. team. And what's our proof? A wrinkled piece of paper that anyone could have written on. The only people who'd have backed us up are gone.'

'And I can't think that Wallenstein and his flunkies will be very happy with us for trying to crack the stone wall they set up,' Andy pointed out. 'Besides, it's just virtual guns – it's not like they've got an armory in their hotel room. If this becomes public knowledge, half the teams will probably be kicking themselves that they didn't come up with the trick.'

'Yeah,' David said in a flat voice. 'It's just a game – just for fun. Until the C.A. team wins and they get their hands on technology our government's been denying them for two decades.' He dug a piece of paper from his pocket. 'Just for fun, I tried a Net search on any Cetniks, cross-referenced with higher education in cybernetics. It's not a very popular name in the Balkans, I guess. There were only a few hits. I printed out this one.'

It was the record of a Slobodan Cetnik, a student in cybernetics at the Polytechnic at Cetinje before the last blowup in the Balkans.

'The age is probably right,' Leif said.

'And that picture looks like him if you add a mustache,' Matt added.

'Your ID picture would look like him if we added a mustache,' Andy retorted. 'We can't tell anything for sure.'

'Then if we can't do anything in the real world, can we do anything to protect ourselves in veeyar?' Leif asked.

David brightened a little. This was an area he could handle. 'I was thinking of trying something with the force-fields.'

'It takes a lot of juice to shrug off an energy weapon – even a laser,' Matt objected. 'We'd probably have to shut down everything to generate a field that could protect us. And then we'd become a sitting duck. If the Thuriens kept pecking away, they'd nail us sooner or later.'

'I was thinking more along the lines of an offensive weapon,' David replied. 'The fields are just generated energy patterns. If we extended our hyperspace sails to touch another ship, would that give us enough conductance to send along a more powerful zap?'

Leif ran his mind over the emitters for the energy sails. 'The projectors would give us a decent enough field of fire,' he said slowly. 'But I don't think we could generate enough power to blow a hole in them.'

'No, I don't think we could blow their airlocks off,' David said. 'But we may put their eyes out. Could we generate enough of a surge to blow their scanners? If they can't see, they can't shoot.'

The continued working on that contingency scheme until late into the night.

The next morning, Leif was the first up.

What goes around, comes around, he thought. *I was the last up yesterday.*

He padded around the room, washed up, and crept down for some breakfast.

The early-morning business crowd had just about cleared the hotel's dining room when Leif came in. And since this was supposed to be a free day for the contestants, most seemed to prefer catching a few more Zs.

Then Leif spotted Ludmila in a corner of the room. She had a fully loaded tray from the breakfast buffet and didn't appear to be touching any of it.

Grabbing some juice, milk, cereal, and a banana, he walked over to join her.

'Hello, Leif.' Ludmila's greeting seemed quiet, lackluster – no dimples today.

'I'm usually not up this early, degenerate American that I am,' he told her.

That got him at least the ghost of a smile. 'So, the *domovina*'s propaganda is right.'

'I suppose you're always up early, feeding the chickens or something.'

Ludmila sat up very straight. 'We do have cities in the Alliance, you know,' she said. 'My mother and I live in one. She works in a factory.'

'And your father?'

She shook her head. 'Dead in the war.' For a long moment, her eyes seemed to focus on nothing. 'By this time in the day back home, my mother would already be off to work. I get up to have breakfast with her – to have some time with her. And between the time when she leaves and school . . . I have time alone.'

'What do you do?' Leif asked.

Ludmila shrugged. 'Read, study sometimes. Early morning was my designing time for our ship's engines.'

And the ship's weapons? Leif wondered.

'But often enough, I use the time to daydream,' the girl went on, looking a little embarrassed. Then she looked as if she'd come down to earth with a thud. 'But what we dream of, and the reality – those are two different things.'

Leif frowned slightly, trying to understand her mood. 'I'm afraid you're losing me, Ludmila.'

She looked at him, a very direct stare from blue eyes under flaxen eyebrows. 'What was your first experience of virtual reality?'

'Veeyar?' The question seemed to come out of left field. 'I don't know. I was pretty young at the time.' Even then, his parents had had enough money to afford the best systems available. Leif tried hard to recall. 'Maybe it was some sort of toddler's fantasyland. I seem to remember a big, pink bunny who played games with me. It might have been a cartoon character come to life.' He felt color rising in his face. 'If I remember right, it sort of scared me. I was howling for my mother.'

Ludmila actually laughed and ruffled his hair. 'Afraid? A clever, fox-like fellow like you? That's what I should call you – *lisica*, the fox.'

She suddenly yanked her hand away, as if she'd burnt it.

161

'Sorry. I shouldn't have done that,' she said.

I wasn't complaining, Leif thought.

'Shall I tell you about my first time in – what did you call it? Veeyar? How very American to slur it all together.' Her face grew very still. 'I was four years old when the training started – the training all the children of Savez Karpaty receive. It's an annual training simulation – what to do if the *domovina* were invaded by aggressor states. I cried, too, as I was herded along past burning buildings, through smoke, away from explosions. We were taught how to get off a road quickly in case aircraft came to strafe, how to step aside for our own forces' tanks and trucks.'

'And you had to do this every year?' Leif said.

Ludmila nodded. 'Just before spring – the start of campaigning season. Year by year, my duties changed. As a little one, I was a despised *nestrovik* – a noncombatant.' Her lips puckered, as if tasting the word. 'Odd. It doesn't sound half as awful in English.'

'What did you do?' Leif asked.

He received a shrug in answer. 'My job was to stay out of the way of our defenders and not to be captured by the enemy. Then I grew older, and received more responsibility. I had to guide the younger children, to lead them away from the fighting as I had been led when I was smaller.'

She smiled, but there were tears in her eyes. 'I'll bet I've wiped more virtual noses than you've kissed girls.'

'Real or virtual?' Leif asked, trying to lighten the moment.

'Both,' Ludmila replied seriously. 'The bigger I got, the more jobs I could do. I was taught about first aid and fighting fires – things I suppose you learn with your Net Force Explorers. We learned things we had to practice between simulations. And all the time, we had it drummed into our heads – ours was a country in arms, where everyone must be ready to work, to fight . . . in whatever capacity the *domovina* required.'

'And who was supposed to invade you?' Leif wanted to know. The last war had been started when Alliance factions had tried to seize land and drive off the inhabitants.

'Oh, we had all sorts of invaders over the years,' Ludmila said quietly. 'Sometimes it was the troops of nearby countries – wherever the tensions were greatest. They would plunder, take hostages, kill civilians like me. The programmers made the wounds hurt, to teach us a lesson.'

Leif winced. He'd encountered virtual bullets like that.

'Other times, the invaders were aggressors from the European Union, or the United Nations – they would program African troops to frighten us – cruel, like animals.'

Never miss a chance for a little propaganda, Leif thought.

'But in every simulation, sooner or later, the Americans would come. And they'd be the worst of all, bombing us, blowing up buildings, leaving scorched earth where there had been farms and homes. Destroying our land just to prove to the world that they had the power to do it.'

Leif looked at the girl in silence. *If I had been brought up all my life in that sort of madhouse*, he wondered, *what kind of feelings would I have about this country?*

'I hope we've been able to show you that Americans aren't like that,' he said.

Ludmila only shook her head, her eyes focused far beyond him again. He could only wonder what she was seeing there.

'This year I was "promoted," as they say, to combat.' Her voice was very brittle. 'We had target practice, and learned to crawl around in the mud – the basic training.

But this was our test of fire. It's almost funny. We fought African troops . . . and Americans . . .'

Her words trailed away. And at last, understanding hit Leif like a bolt of lightning.

Who would operate the weapons on a racer?

On armed explorers, star cruisers like the *Constellation*, the combat command console played an important part on the bridge. It could double for other damaged bridge locations, and the combat commander – the redoubtable Commander Konn – operated the ship's weapons.

But the racers were down to the smallest possible crews. A captain to make the crucial decisions. A scanning officer to keep an eye on everything around him. A helm officer to lay courses, steer, and take evasive maneuvers if necessary. They were all too busy to fire a gun. That left the engineer, Leif's job . . . and Ludmila's.

For the glory of the *domovina*, Ludmila had gunned down the Setangi craft, robbing the African crew of their chance to a fair race. She'd done what she was supposed to do, but she was human enough to feel guilty about it. Obviously, she didn't like the killing, even in veeyar.

What can I tell her? Leif suddenly thought of the hundreds of hours he'd spent in dogfights, showdowns, war games, and the thousand and one ways of 'playing guns' in the world of simulation. He felt a little small.

Then a more disquieting thought hit him. Ludmila had mentioned fighting Africans and *Americans* in veeyar. One part of those 'dreams' had become reality. Was she trying to warn him about the other?

'Ludmila,' he began.

She only gasped, staring over his shoulder as if she saw Death standing in the distance.

Chapter Seventeen

Leif risked a casual glance over his shoulder – and saw Mr Cetnik standing at the entrance to the restaurant, scanning the tables.

'What?' He turned back to Ludmila, but she was no longer in her seat. She'd ducked beneath the table, hiding behind the tablecloth. Her eyes were pleading. 'I was ordered not to talk to you,' she whispered.

Great, Leif thought. *If he glances over here and notices this is a table for two . . .*

Reaching across the table, he grabbed up Ludmila's untouched plate, moved his empty cereal bowl in its place, and began choking down cold eggs, bacon, and sausage. He wasn't really a breakfast eater – the effort made him feel a little queasy.

But he was able to turn back to Cetnik with a full mouth and a legitimate claim to the monster meal on the table. 'Ah!' he said genially, nodding to the C.A. agent. 'No better way to start the day!'

He even managed a mild burp.

It worked. Cetnik turned away from the degenerate American in disgust. He obviously didn't spot Ludmila where she crouched. Instead, he stomped off toward the locker room for the pool and the hotel's health club.

Ludmila looked up at him with shining eyes. 'Oh!' she breathed patting his knee. 'You *are* a *lisica*! A clever fox!'

Then she was out of her hiding place and leaving the restaurant. Wherever Cetnik found her, she would be far from the redheaded American boy.

Leif picked up his napkin to wipe his lips and blot up the sudden dampness on his palms.

For a girl I only met a couple of days ago and have every reason to distrust, this is getting intense, he thought.

He also knew that he had to see her again. She had been on the verge of telling him about something her team was up to, until Cetnik turned up and scared her away. So in spite of what Comrade Cetnik wanted, Leif would have another talk with Ludmila Plavusa.

Just as Leif was about to get up and head back to his suite, the other members of his team entered the restaurant.

'There you are!' Matt greeted him with a grin. 'We thought you'd been kidnapped.'

'Transmatted away,' Andy added, with an appropriate *oooooh-wheeee-ooooooh* sound effect.

Leif shook his head. 'There's something unhealthy about people who are this cheerful so early in the day.'

Even David had to smile. 'You look like you should have had breakfast with Mr Mustache. Cetnik's walking around with a face like he mistook the vinegar bottle for his flask of *slivovitz*.'

'He's afraid one of his team members is up to individual instead of mass action,' Leif said, stealing the slogans of the radical anarcho-libertarians. He pitched his voice lower. 'I think Ludmila was trying to warn me about something, but he turned up and scared her off.'

'Yeah, right,' Andy said in cheerful disbelief. 'She's

fallen for your manly sophistication.'

'I think it was more my after-shave,' Leif replied. 'But seriously, I think something is up.'

Matt rolled his eyes. 'What next? Are these guys going to start dropping antimatter mines on the ships that are too close behind them?'

'What exactly did she say?' David pressed.

Leif didn't know how to answer. If he gave the full story, the guys would probably blow it off. So he edited – considerably. 'She was talking about how the Carpathian Alliance trains its kids almost from infancy to be ready for an invasion. And as they grow older, they're taught to fight the invaders.'

'Pretty cool,' Andy said.

Leif was reminded of Captain Winter's comment over the phone – the one about kids thinking they're immortal until their first firefight. *Here's one who's never gotten past playing guns,* he thought.

'Anyway, the last sim she was in was combat against U.N. peacekeepers from Africa – and Americans. Since she had to be the gunner on the sword-ship, it just made me think—'

'What?' Andy jibed. 'That she's gonna gun us down next?'

'There's the Laragant ship ahead of us,' Matt said.

David concentrated on the practical problem. 'Good figuring. Of course, she'd have to be operating the weapons system.' Then he frowned. 'I just wish you'd found out something a little more solid.'

'You and me both,' Leif told him. 'I'm going to try and track her down. But for this next sequence, we'd better be ready for anything.'

'Yeah.' Andy looked back as he and the others trooped

over to the buffet. 'That should narrow down our worries a bit.'

Leif spent the rest of the day in search of Ludmila. But she was nowhere to be found – probably in the suite reserved for Mr Cetnik and the Carpathian Alliance team. She did come out to the pool in the afternoon and ate in the restaurant that evening, but each time she was surrounded by her teammates. Zoltan, the team's captain, developed a murderous scowl on his face whenever Leif got within twenty yards of the girl.

Ludmila's expression just silently asked Leif not to cause trouble.

Defeated, Leif finally went up to his room and looked longingly at his bed. Well, maybe just a couple of minutes to rest his eyes . . .

The next thing he knew, Andy was roughly shaking his shoulder. 'Wakey-wakey! David said you looked so sweet there, zonking off, he didn't have the heart to disturb you. But we're supposed to be driving over to the studio this evening, and that means we've got to be starting soon.'

Leif flopped around on the bedspread for a moment. Dropping off had been a bad idea. He felt almost drunk – or drugged. Struggling to his feet, he shambled off to the bathroom to throw cold water in his face.

He felt a little better as they drove over to the studio. But he was still clumsy – his hands felt as if they were a size too large.

Wonderful, he thought. *Just wonderful. Tonight we've got to do the fan dance with our force-sails, and I'm bumping into things like a stumblebum.* The proposed scene would be a real test for the racers' engineers. They'd have to transfer in hyperspace from the current they were riding to another

current that would taken them on their way more quickly.
Those who succeeded would build up a nearly unbeatable
lead. Those with engineers who were all thumbs might as
well have stayed home.

When they arrived at Casa Falldown, Leif went straight
to the bathroom for more cold water on the face. He also
let it run over his wrists.

Pull yourself together, he told himself sternly. *Your mom is
a ballet dancer. You can handle this.*

Then he knocked over the pile of paper napkins left on
the basin in place of towels.

'Glad you could make it,' Andy said when Leif joined
the team in its little office. They were already set in their
computer-link couches. 'What happened? You trip over
one of the bundles of wires?'

Leif pushed back the stab of annoyance as he dropped
into his couch. 'I'm here now,' he said. 'Let's get on with
it.'

A moment after synching in, he was on the bridge of the
Onrust.

David spun round his command chair to look at him.
'You okay, Leif?'

'Yeah,' Leif answered. 'But the next time we do this,
don't let me nap so close to show time.'

He felt more and more with it as the time before the
scene ticked away.

Adrenaline, he thought, *still the world's best natural fog-
cutter.*

Leif examined the situation frozen on the forward viewscreen. Two vessels – the Thurien ship like a sharp dagger
and the graceful Laragant quadship – hung before them,
the soap-bubble shimmer of their force-sails extended to
their full glory. Shortly ahead, however, the current they

were following kinked, and the river of force moved away at an angle from the planet that was their target.

But there was another current ahead and to the right, lost in the roiling grayness of hyperspace, that could take a vessel to their destination even faster than they were moving now. The trick was to hit the sharp turn, twist the sails to throw them off the current at the correct angle, shift power from the sails to scanning so they could find their next ride, and then deploy the sails to catch that current.

Simple. Ninety-seven things to do in almost as little time as it took to describe them. Of course, they were programmed into the computer, so that all he had to do was hit a button at the right time. Given that every ship would be trying to do exactly the same thing at exactly the same place, they'd left the initiation of the sequence under manual control. Surely he could manage to push that button at the right time, even in his present state . . .

Leif ran damp palms down the seams of his uniform trousers. *Hands, don't fail me now.*

The lights dimmed, and Hal Fosdyke asked the ship's captains to sound off. Then he announced the countdown . . . and the world on the viewscreen came to life again.

Ahead of them, the Thurien sword-ship suddenly slewed round, her force-fields flickering wildly as they moved in a complex pattern to make the most of the current's momentum.

Then came the Laragants, moving in the same intricate dance.

'Engineering?' David asked.

'Ready,' Leif replied.

'We're coming up,' both Matt and Andy chorused, eyes

flicking from their consoles to the viewscreen. Leif studied his own readouts, his fingers ready to dance across the necessary controls.

'Deploy!' David ordered.

'Deploying.' Leif ran the program to haul them halfway through the turn and then onto their own private parabola through the hyper-dimensions. His eyes were only on his displays, monitoring the exact stresses and speeds being exerted on each sail, his fingers making minute adjustments to their trim.

Only when they were fully free of the current, the sails down and the power now transferred to Scanning, did he look at the viewscreen again. 'Are we on course' he asked.

Andy didn't answer. He was staring at the sword-ship ahead of them. The sword-ship whose sails hadn't gone down. Instead, they began to surge and flare, giant auroras rippling through the spectrum.

'What's going on?' Matt asked. 'Some kind of malfunction?'

'Engineering?' David asked.

'It's like no configuration I've ever seen,' Leif began.

As if to underscore his words, the grossly overblown sails began increasing in brightness, an eye-searing chromatic display that began to pulsate. No. It was blinking. Blinking at an incredibly fast pace, but definitely blinking. As he tried to shield his eyes, his arm seemed to rise in the choppy motion of bad stop-motion animation. Like the old-time rock bands and their strobe lights . . .

A queasy feeling expanded in his gut, as if the floor beneath his feet were sliding off at a steep angle. Leif found himself clinging to his console as the only solid rock in a suddenly dizzy universe.

What was going on?

Suddenly Leif remembered a party, an older gentleman telling his father about early computer animation. A flat-screen Japanese TV show that had been pulled off the air well before the turn of the century because the strobe effects in the computerized explosions had caused seizures very much like epilepsy. But every holo and veeyar system in the world had safeguards to keep it from happening again. So what was going on here? No telling, only that it was happening again, safeguards or no.

'Kill the screens!' Leif screamed. 'Matt!'

Leif was trying not to look at the blazing spectacle winking away at him. But the impact seemed even able to penetrate his closed eyelids.

Leif lurched from his station, grabbing for the command chair to keep upright. David lay half-slumped over, his whole body quivering.

Matt was out, too. Andy was trying to get up, but he couldn't seem to get his muscles to work together.

Facing the empty space between David's chair and Matt's was like looking down the Grand Canyon, a horrifying, long drop that made Leif's stomach and brain spin with vertigo. He took each step with a wooden clomping tread. It felt as if somebody had greased the soles of his shoes. Every time he moved a foot, he was sure it was going to slide out from under him. And if he fell, he knew he'd never get up.

Somehow, he made it to Matt's workstation. His friend was lolling over the console. Leif seized his shoulder and nearly threw himself down on the floor trying to move Matt away.

Don't let me miss, he silently begged.

His finger came down on the correct contact. The sensory barrage lifted, as if someone had stopped beating

The Great Race

him over the head with the world's largest, toughest water
balloon.

The room was silent, except for someone making an
awful choking sound deep in his throat. At last Leif
realized that person was himself.

Matt came round, wiping a smear of drool from his
chin. 'Wh-what was that?' he croaked.

'Tell you later.' Leif's voice wasn't that much better.
'But there's no way it should have been able to happen.
Can you put up the schematic view rather than the real
image?'

On the show, the scanners could deliver different kinds
of displays. When they were damaged, or there was spatial
interference, or just because the writers wanted them to,
the screens could show a radar-type image.

There was certainly enough interference out there now, Leif
told himself. *Any more and it would have fried my brain.*

The little blips crawling across the phosphorescent
background told the story. The sword-ship, no longer
displaying the glorious wings of death in this screen
format, was smoothly following the arc of its chosen orbit
to catch the next hyperspace current. So was the *Onrust*.

But the Laragant ship was going astray. Perhaps the
sickening stroboscopic beat had already affected the vessel's
engineer as they shot off their old current. Maybe suddenly
spastic hands had made a disastrous maladjustment. The
Laragants were adrift. They'd never catch the new current.
They'd have to drop out of hyperspace and find a new
current that would take them where they wanted to go.
Unless they found that current fast, they were out of the
race.

The ships behind them were in even worse shape. A
stylized cloud expanded where ships four and five should

be. They'd apparently collided. Some were still trying to make the jump. Others had failed even to leave the first current. They were being drawn around the sharp turn, dragged along on an expensive detour.

Leif had managed to stumble back to David, who was trying to push himself up. He stared at the screen. 'Can we still make it?'

Even as they watched, the Thurien blip suddenly jerked, caught in the new current.

'They can't be screwing around with the sails now,' Leif said. At least, he hoped so.

Matt tried the real-time image, his hand poised to snap them back to schematic if that lethal pulse was still beating at them.

No. Leif lurched to his action station. They still might make it . . .

'Spotted the current,' Matt gasped. A faint glow on the screen indicated their target.

'Conjunction – five seconds,' Andy said from the helm.

'Engineering?' The single word seemed to cost David a mighty effort. He listed in his chair afterwards.

'Can do,' Leif said, resuming his station.

'Deploy!' David's voice was a hoarse whisper.

'Deploying.' Leif punched in the start of the sequence, and the force-sails sprang into being.

If they catch, we're on our way. Otherwise . . . there was no hope he'd be able to tweak the deployment as fast as he needed to in his current shape.

They swung round, following the Thurien vessel at the same high speed.

Leif sagged against his console. They'd done it!

The scene on the viewscreen suddenly froze. No blinking of lights, no word of warning.

174

A voice did speak, but it didn't belong to Hal Fosdyke. 'Simulation will cease in five seconds. Please disengage. Simulation will cease in four seconds.'

The last thing they needed after this was to go through a systems crash. Leif and his friends cut their connections . . . and found themselves in bedlam.

Horrible, bubbling screams echoed down the halls. The sound – and smell – of someone losing their lunch assailed them. There were thumps, and bumps – and the ominous sound of someone's feet drumming on the floor.

Leif pushed himself off the computer-link couch and moved to the door. He moved about as fast as if he were carrying the couch on his back.

The damage from the pulsing flare hadn't been confined to their virtual selves. It had apparently attacked the senses and nerves of all the synched-in racers!

It could be worse, Leif realized. Fosdyke and his crew had the scene up in holo, watching it unfold and marking angles of presentation. Would the display version of those murderous wings have the same effect?

Sirens howled in the distance as the Net Force Explorers picked their way around the cable-strewn floors of Casa Falldown. The name seemed horribly appropriate as they moved shakily into other offices to offer what help they could. Almost everybody in the building had fallen down – and most of them couldn't get up.

Leif stood in the blessed darkness outside, taking deep breaths of the freshest air Los Angeles had to offer. His head still ached, and an occasional tremor would hit his hands, but he felt considerably better than he had. The boys had waved in the first paramedics to arrive – there were much more serious cases in need of aid still inside.

But as the situation calmed down, he and his friends had submitted to examinations and gotten at least conditional bills of health.

They they'd hiked over to the administration building to call for a cab. No way were they going back into the house of horrors that was now Casa Falldown.

Most of the contestants were on their way to the hospital. A stream of stretchers was also coming out of the special-effects building, where Hal Fosdyke and his people had indeed been felled.

The biggest surprise came as Leif and his friends faced the office building. Several stretchers came out of the main entrance, surrounded by anxious paramedics.

The twitching, bulky form on the lead gurney was unmistakable.

It was Milos Wallenstein!

Chapter Eighteen

The producer had the most paramedics of any patient Leif had seen, and he didn't think they were treating Wallenstein by the pound.

Of course, a cynical voice whispered in the back of his head, *maybe he's getting the Hollywood producer treatment. Or maybe some of the paramedics are Fronties.*

But one of the emergency medics looked very worried as he checked the still-quivering fat man. 'He's having a particularly bad reaction.'

Leif, David, and Andy looked at one another. 'Maybe it's the shaking-up my brain got a little earlier,' Andy said, 'but this is making less and less sense to me.'

'To us too, I think,' Leif said. 'Right now, I don't want to discuss it. I don't even want to think about it.'

David nodded. 'bed sounds better and better to me.'

Matt rejoined them, saying that he'd arranged for the cab to pick them up at the main gate. They walked down in silence, too drained to talk about anything.

A new problem confronted them before they could get some rest, however. The media had gotten wind of some sort of disaster at Pinnacle Studios, and had turned out like a flock of vultures. News photographers clustered across the street, snapping shots of police cars entering and ambulances leaving. The emergency vehicles could scarcely move because of the news vans pulling up – both local stations and national holo-nets.

Tiredly, Leif turned to Matt. 'Do you remember the name of that cab company the receptionist called? Maybe we can divert it to another gate.'

They arrived back at the hotel like thieves in the night, heading straight to their suite – and discovering an urgent call from Captain Winters.

Leif found himself elected spokesman, and he decided this call was better conducted in full holo format, with the others standing behind him. As soon as the captain saw them, he began shooting off questions in a full military bark.

'We've gotten some very contradictory reports through the media,' he said. 'I want the real facts.'

As Leif explained, backed by technical details from Matt and David, Winter's stony expression grew even more grim. 'An unknown number of civilians injured by means of hologram. I suppose we should be thankful that it didn't happen during a general broadcast.'

Leif didn't see anything to be added to that sentiment.

The captain slammed his hands down on his desk. 'This has gotten well beyond youthful hijinks! I'm recommending that we take off the gloves with Pinnacle Productions. Up to this point, their legal department has been giving us the runaround. Personal privacy, proprietary systems – the only thing they haven't invoked is the separation of church and state. But their lawyers can't shrug this off. Somebody got around the safety protocols both for the Net and for holo-net broadcast. That's not the work of some kid in his garage – or goat shed.'

Winters had the look of a man who thought he'd picked up a rope and discovered instead that it was a tiger's tail. 'We're talking elaborate, layered protections. Sometimes a bright programmer can get around them to the extent of giving someone a mild shock.'

Leif thought about David and his punitive crash program.

'But circumventing the safeties to this extent requires the resources of a major corporation . . . or government.' Winters glared out at his young men. 'Rest assured, we *will* find out who did it.'

He cut the connection, and with his words still ringing in their ears, the boys staggered off to bed.

They slept like dead men, awakening the next morning with barely enough time to get down to the restaurant before breakfast was over. The dining room was very sparsely occupied. Most of the contestants who'd normally be eating at this time were getting breakfast in the hospital.

Of course, one team sat at a central table, looking like a sullen family group – the extremely unpopular bunch from the Carpathian Alliance. Both Zoltan and Mr Cetnik glowered at the Net Force Explorers as they came in, glares of hatred as intense as laser blasts. Leif was glad they weren't in veeyar. He and his friends would be on the floor with holes burnt through them.

He also noticed that Ludmila looked as if she hadn't slept a wink all night.

The Net Force Explorers got their food and took it to a table as far as possible from the C.A. team.

'All right,' Andy said. 'I've kept my mouth shut since we got up. But I've got to ask. What were they thinking to pull the nonsense they did last night?'

'I think they saw a chance to seize an unbeatable lead . . . and they took it.' David took a sip of weak tea, tore a bit of crust off the dry toast he'd taken, and began chewing.

Of the four of them, only Andy, the human garbage can, had loaded up a full platter. Just the smell of all that food made Leif faintly queasy.

'If that's what they hoped for, we must be breaking their hearts,' Matt said, his eyes on his cereal bowl. 'We're still on their tail.'

Leif nodded. *No wonder we got those looks when we came in,* he thought. *They went way beyond the lines of gamesmanship this time.* Pranks, even sabotage, were one thing. But the latest exploit of Cetnik & Co. had put people in the hospital. It had drawn the attention of the media. And most galling from the Alliance's point of view, it hadn't gotten them what they wanted.

'I can see what they were aiming for,' Andy said around a mouthful of scrambled eggs. 'But was it worth it? I mean one of the people on the stretchers was Milos Wallenstein. We always figured he was their friend at the studio.'

'That's right,' Matt chimed in. 'Look at the way he placated Cetnik for the press conference, and covered for the C.A. team's spying and sabotage.'

'Not to mention hiding the fact that their ship is armed,' Leif added dryly. 'We thought the big guy's politics were influencing his better judgment on the first few incidents. And we thought that maybe he'd been caught off guard when the Thuriens used their guns. Maybe he got a worse surprise last night. I can't believe that anybody would risk exposing themselves to that killer light show if they'd been warned in advance.'

'Could have been a technical slipup,' David suggested.

'They might have thought the strobe effect would only nail people in veeyar, that it wouldn't be a problem in holo-form.'

Matt looked deeply suspicious. 'Or he could have suffered through it to look innocent.'

'So depending on which case you believe, Wallenstein would have to be a true fanatic, or a tool who could be dispensed with once he'd been use,' Leif said. 'One thing's for sure, though. His job is at risk after last night.'

The other three boys stared at him. 'Think about it.' Leif spread out his hands. 'He exposed the studio to a slew of lawsuits – and for what? A special-effects holo that can never be shown without literally giving the audience fits.'

They finished their breakfast under another set of unfriendly gazes – the restaurant staff was eager to get the room set up for lunch. When the Net Force Explorers returned to their room, the housekeeper was just leaving.

'Excuse me, sir,' she said as she moved her cleaning cart through the door. 'I think there's a message on your console.'

Leif stepped inside. Sure enough, the display on the room's holo-suite was glowing on and off. He immediately ordered the computer to kill it – they had all had enough of blinking lights just now – and asked for the message to be displayed.

'Hey, guys,' he called. 'There's a message from Pinnacle Studios. We got some good news – and some interesting news.'

The others joined him to read the brief note. 'I'm glad that everybody should be out of the hospital by this afternoon,' David said.

Andy pointed at the final paragraph. 'But what do you

think they're going to say at the press conference they've scheduled?'

'We'll find out when we get there,' Leif said. 'The bus is supposed to pick us up at one.'

The ride out to Pinnacle Studios took place in almost total silence. Most of the contestants, newly released from observation in the hospital, were not in a talkative mood. And all of them were angry to be riding with the team who'd put them in the hospital in the first place. There was a cordon of empty seats around the team from the Carpathian Alliance. It could almost serve as a dictionary definition of the term 'pariah state.'

Even Andy couldn't find something to kid about in the oppressive atmosphere.

The C.A. kids bailed out of the bus quickly, followed by the other teams. They were herded into the same oversized screening room where Wallenstein had heralded the beginning of the race just a few days ago.

It was a different Milos Wallenstein who greeted the kids today. He looked sick – and somehow deflated, Leif thought, as if the events of last night had somehow shrunk him.

If anything, the press turnout was even larger than for the race kickoff.

Of course, Leif thought. *Now they've got some kind of scandal to cover*. Not that he expected in-depth coverage on the broadcast news. How many holo-nets were going to tell their audiences that watching holograms could be bad for their health if somebody messed with their computer?

Wallenstein's usually booming voice had to be amplified to fill the room this time. 'Ladies and gentlemen of the press, contestants, and fans. While recording a sequence for our Great Race episode last night, we – myself included – suffered a considerable mishap. Since the racing sequences are completely unscripted, anything could occur. What happened might be considered beyond the bounds of competition – the lead team used a pulsating stroboscopic effect to distract the other racers during a difficult maneuver.

'Unfortunately, this distraction proved all too effective, creating seizure-like symptoms both for the competitors in VR – and for the crew and staff watching the sequence in holoform. However, my technical director, Hal Fosdyke, assures me that with careful editing, the sequence can be used in complete safety for the audience – and with considerable dramatic effects.'

Right, Leif thought, *after Fosdyke and his people completely reanimate it.*

An angry buzz began among the contestants. They'd expected to hear that the lethal recording would have to be scrapped, which would mean an effective do-over of the transfer between hyperspace currents.

Wallenstein underscored his meaning with his next words. 'The results of last night's race sequence will stand.'

The usually pink-faced Danish captain looked more gray today – except for the sudden, hectic flush on his cheeks. 'You mean those *tyven* – those thieves – will be rewarded for what they did?' he burst out.

The producer was obviously ready for such a question.

'It's not a case of sportsmanship,' Wallenstein said carefully, 'but rather of authenticity. The actions of the Thurien team were totally in character for members of that race as they have been portrayed in the series for years.'

In other words, Leif silently translated, *we should have expected lethal tricks from them.*

'One of the hallmarks of the *Ultimate Frontier* series from its inception has been our willingness to go beyond the expected in our treatment of alien races. We want to show the diversity humanity can encounter in the universe – different races, different cultures . . . different ethics.

'We do not condone the actions of an extremely competitive team. But we recognize that their response was a valid manifestation of the diversity of the *Ultimate Frontier* universe – a diversity which all participants were aware of when they agreed to participate in the race. For those who have lost their chances for further competition, we offer our grateful thanks for a splendid effort. For those still in the race – good luck!'

With those words, the producer abruptly left the podium, staggering slightly as he left the room, ignoring the hectoring questions of the media people and the furious comments from the disqualified contestants.

Leif looked after the man almost in sympathy. Looking past all the philosophy he'd spouted, Wallenstein had been forced somehow to let the race play out as it had.

His show is a creature of publicity, Leif thought. *And now he's stuck with the publicity the C.A. stunt created.*

As the Net Force Explorers exited the screening room, Leif dug his hand into his pocket. Out it came with the keys to their rental car. 'I don't know about you guys, but I don't think I could stand much more of that bus.'

David nodded. 'Especially with the mood people will be in now.'

Telling the publicity person responsible for the bus that they'd be taking their own transportation, they headed off for the parking lot. Leif drove out of the gate, but turned in the opposite direction from the one that would take them back to the hotel.

'What are you doing?' Matt asked.

'I thought maybe we could do with some lunch – and I happen to know that there's a drive-in out this way that still serves real hamburgers.'

The place was a drive-in, but it wasn't cheap. Leif used his credit card to get some real food into his teammates. *Call it therapy,* he thought.

Happily full, they headed back along the boulevards to their hotel. As the boys got out, Leif happened to notice the fuel gauge. 'Go on up,' he said. 'I'll go and feed the car, too.'

There was a gas station a few blocks from the hotel. About halfway there, Leif pulled up for a red light – and noticed a familiar figure on the corner. He hit the 'down' button for the passenger-side window. 'Hey, cutie,' he called. 'Need a ride?'

Ludmila Plavusa glanced over in surprise, gave him a happy smile, then looked uneasy. 'I had to get away for a while,' she said. 'I couldn't stand staying around in there with all those people hating us.'

'You won't get very far on foot,' Leif said.

'Mr Cetnik – he uses our car,' Ludmila said stiffly.

'Well, I'm going to the gas station. Want to come along?'

She looked at him almost shyly. 'You wouldn't . . . mind?'

Leif shook his head. 'Come on,' he said.

He unlocked the door and she got in, strapping on the seat belt. Ludmila's blond hair stirred in the slight breeze that came through the window as the car started up.

Well, you wanted to talk with her again, a little voice

pointed out from the back of Leif's mind. *Now's your chance.*

He stopped at the gas station and filled the tank. While the fuel glugged away, Leif got out his wallet-phone and punched in the number for the Net Force Explorers' suite at the hotel. 'Something's come up,' he said quietly as David answered the call. 'I'm going to be out for a little while.'

'We were going to go over other countermeasures to protect ourselves in the final sequence,' David reminded him.

'They're not going to record that tonight, are they?' Leif asked.

'No,' David said. 'There was a message waiting for us when we got back. And I checked in with Jane Givens, just in case it turned out to be a phony. They're giving us a day off before trying to wrap it all up.'

'You're developing a terrible suspicious streak, double-checking messages like that,' Leif teased.

'Must be the people I'm hanging around with,' David retorted.

'Well, you, Matt, and Andy are better at virtual engineering than I am.'

'Yeah,' David said dryly. 'We'll carry you – this time.'

They disconnected, and Leif slipped away his wallet just as the gas pump finished. He got back in the car.

'What do you say to a real drive?' he asked Ludmila.

'Where?' she asked warily.

'You'd never believe it, but there are still places in the hills where the concrete jungle almost disappears.'

They stopped off to buy what Leif called 'necessary supplies,' like sunscreen, bug goop, and a pair of baseball caps to keep off the sun. 'And so we'll look like

186

tourists,' Leif explained. Sunglasses for Ludmila. Some upscale delicatessen for a picnic lunch. Leif could have done without it, but Ludmila confessed that she was starved.

Then they drove up into the hills, to a park surrounding a reservoir. Above them loomed the world-famous Hollywood sign. 'That's Mount Lee,' Leif said, pointing to the hill crest that backed the giant letters. 'A California friend brought me up here during my first visit. He liked to imagine what the land had been like a hundred fifty years ago, when L.A. was still a small town.'

They walked along a jogging trail, then sat under a tree. Leif drank a soda while Ludmila devoured their supplies.

'The mountains back home aren't like this,' she told him. 'The stone is gray. There's less sunshine.' She gave him a smile. 'And there are very few palm trees.'

They talked about nothing for a while, just personal observations about California and traveling. Then Leif decided to take the plunge. 'The last time I talked with you, I got the feeling you wanted to tell me something – but then you disappeared under the tablecloth. Were you trying to warn me about the killer strobe light?'

Ludmila looked down at her feet. 'I knew they had something,' she said, almost too low to be heard. 'Mr Cetnik was on the phone, and I caught part of what he was saying – boasting about something being one-hundred-percent lethal.'

Leif felt cold even in the brilliant sunshine working its way between the leaves. That didn't sound like the strobe effect, which had incapacitated, not killed.

'I'm so ashamed,' Ludmila said miserably. 'It was bad enough to use our laser in simulation. But to actually hurt people!' She shook her head, as if to make the memories go away. 'This is not why I worked and studied to use computers.'

She shivered, and it seemed the most natural thing in the world for Leif to put his arm around her shoulders. Ludmila snuggled against him, and they sat in silence for a while.

'Ludmila—' he finally said.

She didn't answer. She had fallen asleep.

When Ludmila awakened, the shadows were considerably longer. 'Oh, no,' she said, abashed. 'They'll be wondering where I went.'

'Tell them you got turned around on the streets and got lost,' Leif advised. 'Most of the people on the sidewalks of Beverly Hills are tourists. They wouldn't be able to direct you.'

They returned to the car. In moments, they were back in city traffic. As they approached the hotel, an almost identical car to the one Leif was driving pulled out of the garage.

Ludmila immediately slunk down in her seat. 'Mr Cetnik!'

Leif glanced over at her with a smile, impressed by her chaperon radar.

Then his smile faded. 'I bet he won't recognize you wearing that cap and sunglasses,' he said. 'Let's find out where he's going.'

Cetnik was not one to enjoy city streets. He got on the nearest freeway, followed that concrete ribbon to another, and headed west. 'It can't be too far,' Leif muttered. 'The Pacific Ocean will get in his way.'

The Alliance agent got on the coast highway and contin- ued to his destination – Malibu. He exited from the freeway and headed for the beachfront neighborhood.

Ludmila stared around at the small but obviously expensive houses. 'Who would he know out here?' she wondered.

How about a rich anarcho-libertarian supporter? Leif thought, but kept that to himself.

Cetnik's rental car pulled up at a set of gates which automatically opened for him. The driveway climbed to a house clinging to a hillside. The place was made of teak, glass . . . and money.

Leif stopped on the street below, well away from the gate and its security camera. No name, but there was a small, tasteful address number.

Digging out his wallet again, Leif set the circuitry for phone mode again. He punched a code sequence he'd seen Net Force agents use. It connected to a voice-activated database that, strictly speaking, he shouldn't have been able to use. But hey, he was trying to find out who a foreign agent was visiting. Wasn't that appropriate?

The connection was made, and Leif recited the address. A second later, a computer's silvery voice responded. 'Owner of the address in question – Milos Wallenstein.'

'Oh, ho, ho,' Leif muttered, staring up at the beach house in triumph. There was a quick flash in the picture window, and his satisfaction abruptly curdled. That was the kind of reflection you usually got off lenses – say, a pair of field glasses.

While he'd been tracking Cetnik and Wallenstein through high technology, they might have spotted him the old-fashioned way. Using binoculars, they could have also identified Ludmila.

Leif threw the car into gear.

'Did that tell you whose house that was?' Ludmila asked.

189

'It belongs to Milos Wallenstein,' Leif replied shortly. Right now, he just wanted to get out of there. 'He's a big supporter of the anarcho-libertarian movement. And as you may know, some factions in that movement are very fond of your country.'

They drove back to the hotel in silence, his grim, hers puzzled. 'We may have been spotted back there,' Leif finally admitted. He pulled off the side of the road a couple of blocks from the hotel, next to a line of shops. 'I know this isn't the gentlemanly thing to do, but I think we should arrive at the hotel separately. You might want to go play on your own here, maybe come home with a couple of bags from some tourist traps, and at a later time than I do.'

'I have no money,' she said. 'Mr Cetnik pays for everything.'

'That is something I can remedy.' Leif took out a few bills and handed them to her. 'Tell them your mother saved up to give you money to buy mementos of the trip.'

'They will never believe it, but they can't prove me wrong. If they accuse me of seeing you, I will deny everything!' Ludmila cried. She tore off her cap and glasses as if they were damning evidence and threw them into the car. 'I took a walk and went shopping.'

Leif smiled. 'That's the spirit.'

He watched her until she was safely inside a store. Then he pulled away from the curb and continued on to the hotel. Once inside the parking garage, Leif pulled the car into its assigned space, and got out.

A figure suddenly appeared from behind one of the concrete support pillars – a large, broad, male figure.

Zoltan, the captain of Ludmila's team, stood glaring at him.

Chapter Nineteen

The hulking boy from the Carpathian Alliance moved toward the car. 'So where is our Ludmila?' Zoltan asked.

'I don't know – you're the ones who've been keeping her under lock and key,' Leif replied. 'Did you lose her?'

'Do not deny what I know to be true. You won't like what happens next.'

'Oh?' Leif asked. 'Is this where you set yourself up for a charge of assault?'

'Your smart mouth won't save you now,' Zoltan told him. 'This isn't like the time on the bus with that Corteguayan fool. There are no witnesses.'

He snarled something in his native language as he looked Leif up and down. 'So much crime in these American cities,' he purred, grinding his right fist into his left palm. 'Who will care about one more statistic?'

His smile was confident as he stepped forward. After all, there was enough of him to make two of Leif. 'Perhaps I'll take your wallet, so it will look like a robbery. Or maybe I'll leave it. You look like the type to get on the wrong side of a jealous boyfriend.'

The smile was gone as he turned back to Leif. 'Foolish American,' he said venomously. 'Soft. Decadent. Obsessed with toys. Your time of greatness is long past, yet you sit like a heavy weight on those who would change the world. And your arrogance! Like this foolish show, where you imagine your weak-minded ideal spreading across the galaxy!'

His laugh was like a sharp bark. 'When men got to the stars, they will be more like Thuriens than your weak-kneed Galactic Federation – strong, racially pure warriors!'

Zoltan was almost on Leif now, reaching out with his long arms to grab him. 'I'm going to enjoy this,' he gloated. 'Breaking your – hwuuuuuuuulp!'

Leif took a single step forward, the stiffened fingers of his right hand striking a lance-head just below Zoltan's breastbone and up.

The air gushed out of the bigger guy, and he folded over.

'Not smart, Zoltan,' Leif scolded his adversary, who was still trying to suck into his emptied lungs. 'You were so busy exercising your mouth muscles, you forgot to tighten up your gut. Even a soft, decadent guy like me could nail you in the solar plexus.'

Hunched and gasping, Zoltan tried to grab Leif and crush him in a bear hug. But Leif twisted aside, smashing his hulking opponent in the side of his face with his forearm. Zoltan staggered, and Leif came up behind him, kicking the back of his knee.

Zoltan toppled, hitting the concrete floor hard.

'Man, that's got to hurt,' Leif told him.

The hulking team captain managed to lever himself up on his hands and knees. But he stuck there, his breath still coming in rattling gasps.

Leif stood over him. 'One thing you should bear in mind,' he suggested. 'Net Force Explorers are taught how to handle themselves by U.S. Marines. And while Marines are American, they certainly aren't *soft*!'

He punctuated his message with a looping overhand punch that solidly connected with Zoltan's temple. The big guy keeled over and crashed to the floor again.

This time he didn't seem to be getting up.

And so, we have a demonstration of three important truths, Leif thought as he walked to the elevator.

One, it was better that Ludmila had missed this. She *wouldn't* have liked what she saw.

Two, although it was a cliché, the bigger they come, the harder they *do* fall.

And three, the trainers in Quantico were right. *Never* punch into bone.

Leif kept wiggling his hand, trying to work the pain out of his knuckles, all the way up to the third floor.

'We're so pleased to have your input,' Andy said in annoyance as Leif entered the suite. The Net Force Explorers were in a corner of the living room, working over David's laptop. In the background, a music holo was playing – musicians in drippy green makeup as if their faces were running. A barf-rock band. Leif watched their act for a moment, shaking his head. Doing that all over the audience didn't look like fun to *him*.

'We've been trying to figure out how we're going to survive the end of this race,' Matt pointed out a little testily. He didn't actually come out and accuse Leif of goofing off, but the thought was definitely in there.

'Me, too,' Leif told him curtly. He went to the holo-suite, killed the music, and initiated a call to Captain Winters. 'I've been talking to a member of the C.A. team,' Leif told the captain. 'She believes they've got something worse than that fit-inducer up their sleeves – something lethal.'

The captain's face set in familiar lines – the worry of a commander sending troops into danger. 'I want you to pull the plug,' he said.

Leif couldn't answer, thanks to a storm of protest from the other guys. He waited for his chance. 'Can Net Force shut this down?'

'Pinnacle Productions pays its lawyers well – and they earn their pay,' Winters grimly replied. 'If you had details of this lethal application . . .'

'Captain, I can't even be sure it's for real,' Leif unhappily admitted. 'If you can't stop the race and we pull out, the C. A. wins. And even if you keep them from shipping the stuff home, can you block them from evaluating the equipment for charitable donations?'

'If the Pinnacle lawyers get in the way, it might take time,' Winters didn't like what he was saying, but he told the truth.

'The rule of law,' David said bitterly. 'While the lawyers wrangle, C.A. spies could be dissecting all that cutting-edge technology.'

'That's not my concern. You boys, however, are very much my concern. And I'm not having you put yourselves at risk. These people have already demonstrated that they're willing to do anything to win. I want you to fall behind and stay there once you start the race. In fact – I'd prefer it if you crashed and burned as soon as possible. I want you out of there before there's any possibility of trouble.'

'But, sir . . .' Leif protested.

'You heard me. I'll keep you posted on the lawyers. Now go get some rest. You look like you could use it.' Winters signed off.

As soon as the image faded, Leif looked at his friends.

'Are we going to back down and lose the very thing we've come this far to win?' he asked.

The chorus of protests from everyone in the room made it clear that he wasn't the only one who thought that was a bad idea. 'So we stay in the race, but take every precaution we can think of.'

'What if we run into trouble?' David asked.

'We'll report it immediately,' Leif promised.

If we're alive to do so, a gloomy little voice snickered in his brain. But he wasn't running away like a whipped dog at the first sign of trouble. None of them were.

They went back to the problem at hand.

'Death threats or no death threats, we're the only competition left that's even close to the Thuriens. The other ships are so far back, they'll be breaking out of hyperspace several minutes after we do.'

'And you know what that means,' Matt said grimly. 'No witnesses.'

Where have I just heard that? Leif wondered, heading over to the refrigerator to get some ice for his knuckles.

'The *Constellation* and the other ships are barred from the system until one racer has tagged the finish buoy,' David said, repeating the winning conditions.

'Which means there's nothing to stop the Thuriens from tagging us with their lasers if we even give the suggestion that we can beat them to the buoy.' Andy shrugged. 'What do they need this killer program for?'

'I can only tell you what Ludmila told me,' Leif said. 'She overheard Cetnik talking about another trick they've got up their sleeves. Something one-hundred-percent lethal.'

'Like what?' Matt demanded.

Leif shook his head helplessly. 'She doesn't know.'

David looked at his friend. 'Do you think she's serious, or is this some kind of ploy for information?'

'After what happened to old Jorge from Corteguay, I'd have to say you've got a point,' Leif admitted. He looked around at his friends. 'But I'd say she was serious – and telling the truth. After all, the C.A. team has already shown itself to be pretty inventive – and nasty.'

'They were willing to hurt people,' David agreed. 'But outright murder?'

'Hey, with some of those seizure victims, it could have gone either way,' Andy said. 'Is that so very different?'

'So we've got something else to worry about,' Matt said. 'Well, maybe we should look harder at this emergency mode David's been talking about.'

'What's that?' Leif asked.

'If you'd been here, you'd have heard it from the beginning,' Andy snapped.

'And if I'd been here, the only technical advice I could have given was "make it with a red button or a green button," ' Leif replied. 'You guys are the programming geniuses.'

'Well, it's going to take a lot of work,' David said. 'Essentially, I'm suggesting a way to bail out of the sim but still run it.'

'How?' Leif wanted to know.

'With my little box here.' David patted his lap top computer. 'We'll have to patch it in to the cables connecting the computer-link couches. We'll give up a lot of control, so I haven't suggested it earlier, but then, I'd never have believed a simple contest could get so dangerous. Given the choice between winning and living, I can tell you which side I come down on. So, running things off of my laptop – we won't have the brains to run full simulations, but we can preprogram certain emergency measures. Evasion, full forward thrust—'

'Tagging the finish buoy,' Andy suggested. 'Unfortunately, we won't be able to pull off more complicated stunts, like Project Blindfold.'

Leif managed to keep his face calm. No need to set Andy off again.

'That's one of the countermeasures we discussed the last time,' Matt said, taking pity on his friend. 'Extending our force-sails to knock out their scanners.'

'You found out a way to make it work?' Leif said. 'Great!'

'Yeah – it just took most of the time since we got back here,' Andy said ironically. 'And what have you accomplished?'

'Well, I gassed up the car,' Leif replied. 'I pumped Ludmila for information. And I knocked Captain Zoltan of the Thurien Warfleet flat on his ugly face when he tried to ambush me in the garage.'

'We'll want to hear all about that,' David said in his own captain's voice. 'But first we need to program the emergency measures. Anybody have more suggestions?'

Working up the emergency programs kept the team busy almost to the time they were supposed to leave for recording the big finale. Some parts of their planned countermeasures proved easier said than done. Hours were spent developing the proper program hooks, working from the simple action sims in the hotel system's games files.

If Leif never saw another screen from *Tail Gunner Mario*, it would still be too soon. But when they finished, they were able to send the toy airplane into loop-the-loops and shoot at cartoon pterodactyls while using the keyboard to control it.

Then they graduated to hard games, and more complicated sims, until David pronounced their programming ready for the ultimate challenge. Working over the Net, they accessed the virtual version of the *Onrust* in his home computer and successfully ordered it around.

'This still isn't going to be a walk in the park,' David warned. 'Remember where the finish buoy is located.'

The race developers had come up with one final curveball for the competitors, turning the final buoy into a moving target. And that didn't just mean matching velocities with a simple orbit. No, those sadistic geniuses had placed the buoy in a comet with a shattered nucleus. The teams would actually have to penetrate that mass of grinding space debris and get within a hundred kilometers of the buoy to score a victory.

But that was a concern for the future. Leif's present was devoted to handling all the domestic errands for his friends while their brains ground away at the software problems they had to solve. He did the accumulated laundry, brought in snacks, and even ordered room service to keep them fed through the course of the day. He also talked with a few of the teams that had been eliminated from the race. He was worried about the time the Net Force Explorers would spend in veeyar in this final round. Their actual real-life bodies could be at risk – certainly Zoltan had shown no signs of shyness about wanting to beat him to a pulp. Leif asked members from two of the teams no longer in the race if they'd unobtrusively stand guard over the door to their office at Casa Falldown during the race. Maybe he was getting paranoid, but better paranoid than pulped, he figured.

And while he worked, he worried about Ludmila. He might be stuck as the temporary servant for the duration of the great programming marathon. But she was being kept incommunicado. Most of the time, she seemed to be in the C.A. team's suite. On the rare occasions she came out, Ludmila was always under a teammate's watchful eye. Leif hoped they were unsure enough of her visit with him to refrain from punishing her for it.

She tried to pass you a warning. Leif silently accused himself. *And you got her in deep trouble.*

How could he help her? When the race was over, she'd have to return to her *domovina*, her homeland. It wasn't as though he could offer her asylum. Or that she would accept it, cutting herself off forever from her mother, her family, everything she'd ever known.

It would have been nice to talk to her, just to be sure she was all right. But as they waited for the bus that would take them to Pinnacle Studio for the big showdown, even that small comfort looked pretty unlikely.

When they arrived in the lobby, almost all of the competitors were there. Even the teams who had lost their ships – at least those teams who hadn't been sent home – would watch the final sequence in the large screening room. The kids who had agreed to watch his team's backs nodded at him. It was the predetermined signal that they'd slip out as soon as the race started and keep an eye on things in the real world. Only one team still in L.A. was missing – the pariahs from the Carpathian Alliance.

'The Carpathian Alliance's handler or whatever you call him plans to drive them here in the car,' the Danish captain told the Net Force Explorers.

Leif shrugged. *I hope this isn't a sign of how the rest of the evening will go*, he thought.

★ ★ ★

The halls of Casa Falldown smelled of disinfectant, but despite that, the sour scent of sickness still lingered in the air. David stood in the entrance, his nose wrinkled in disgust.

'However it goes, this will be our last time in here,' Leif said. 'And once we're in virtual mode, we won't be able to smell it.'

David nodded, and they headed to their office. As soon as they were inside, Leif closed the door as far as it could go against the bundle of wires. Matt and Andy pounced on the computer-link chair farthest out of sight from the doorway, yanking the chair's line from its connection in the cable bunch and inserting a shunt wire between the two jacks. They worked quickly and neatly. In almost no time David's computer had been patched into the circuit.

At the moment, it interacted in a passive mode, merely showing what the special-effects department had prepared of the simulation. The computer's display presented a miniature view of the *Onrust*'s bridge. It was really too small to make out what was on the Lilliputian viewscreen. *We'll find out soon enough*, Leif told himself.

If the boys cut their connection with the simulation, however, the laptop's command link would surface, and they would be able to influence their ship's operation from the small computer's keyboard. Specific hot keys had been programmed to launch various maneuvers.

David was still sure that all it would accomplish was crashing them into a chunk of comet-ice.

Better than winding up really dead due to some Carpathian-inspired programming glitch. Leif thought. He was certain that the lethal ace up Cetnik's sleeve would be aimed at the ship most threatening to a Thurien victory. They wouldn't want to kill all the competitors. The crew of the *Onrust* was therefore the most logical target for whatever Cetnik had planned.

As a consequence, Leif's stomach felt tight as he joined his teammates on their computer-link couches and synched in.

A second later, he was on the bridge of the *Onrust*. The roiling gray of hyperspace stood frozen on the viewscreen. Ahead of them was an indistinct shape – the Thurien sword-ship. As for the rear view, no matter how hard Leif examined the viewscreen, he couldn't find a trace of the ships trailing them.

Alone at last, Leif thought. *And they've got the better weaponry*.

The lights dimmed, and Hal Fosdyke's voice asked the contestants to sound off. He sounded a little strained tonight – perhaps he was afraid of new unpleasant surprises being sprung in this session.

They counted down, the viewscreen came to life, and the ships were moving.

'We've got one chance to get ahead of them,' David muttered. 'If we can cut our breakout time even a couple of milliseconds after theirs . . .'

'We'll be deeper into the system and closer to the finish buoy,' Andy finished with him. 'You programmed to breakout – think we can do it?'

'The problem is, we don't know how finely calibrated their breakout software is,' Matt said. 'I've got a manual override programmed in, but I can't predict what their threshold is.'

'Maybe not,' Leif said. 'But the Corteguayans had a better system than theirs – that's who Ludmila was sent after. So we've got a chance.'

They hurtled forward on the strength of the hyperspace current, penetrating deeper into the system. As they reached the end of the breakout envelope, conversation ceased. All eyes were on the irregular blob that represented the Thurien vessel through the distorting grayness of hyperspace.

'Coming close,' Matt muttered.

'Running out of time.' That came from Andy.

Ahead of them, flickers came from the gray blur. 'They've disengaged their sails!' Leif called.

Matt gave a yip. 'They're out of here!'

David was staring with deadly concentration at his armrest readouts. The computer ticked off the last tiny nanoseconds, then initiated the sequence. 'Breakout!' he announced.

The sails deployed, sending them on a new course. The sail power down, warp power up –

The ghostly tail of the comet they were chasing filled most of the forward viewscreen. A tiny dot in the rearview display represented the sword-ship they'd just overshot.

'Andy, lay in the course,' David ordered. 'Maneuver speed on the sublight drive—'

Before his words were finished, a man-sized glow appeared between the scanning and helm consoles. It grew in brightness, was surrounded by a brief corona of energy . . . and solidified into the figure of Commander Dominic. 'Belay that order!' he exclaimed, a smirk on his handsome pirate's face.

The crew members all stared at him. 'What are *you* doing here?' Andy burst out.

'Who are you really?' Leif wanted to know.

'Oh, I'm really me,' Lance Snowdon assured him. 'I'm not here as the good commander, though I'm wearing the uniform. No, I'm Lance Snowdon, actor – and activist. On a little mission for the Carpathian Alliance.'

With that, he aimed the hand-pulser he carried at Matt and pulled the trigger.

The usual blue spark leapt from the weapon's muzzle. It hit Matt even as he struggled from his seat.

And then he dropped like a poleaxed steer across his console.

'Oh, don't worry,' Snowdon assured them as he stepped round to cover them all with his weapon. 'I just hit him with the pulser's knockdown charge. He should be back with us in a moment or two.'

The actors' handsome face smiled at them. 'That's all it will take for the program my Carpathian friends are implanting to disqualify you.'

He nodded at Leif. 'I'm afraid it's going to be your fault, Leif. You won't quite balance the acceleration of the engines. And though you'll keep the ship from tearing itself apart by throwing everything into the hull-stabilization fields, you'll be too far off course to do anything as the Thuriens slip in to claim the prize.'

The man's 'smooth actor' façade was fast disappearing. His eyes burned with an ideologue's fervor. 'And what a prize it will be! A chance to get their hands on some of the finest computer technology available in the world, finer even than any available on the American market today!'

'It won't happen,' Leif told him flatly. 'We've already informed Net Force about that little scam.'

'Then we have to fall back to Plan B,' Snowdon said. 'If we can't get our hands on the technology, we'll carry it off in our brains. Cetnik tells me his little cyber-spies are like sponges, primed to soak up everything they lay eyes on. Maybe then people in Washington will learn that you can't declare embargoes on ideas!'

'Okay,' Andy said, 'We've gone through what and how, so my question is: why?'

'You mean, why turn against our glorious government? Why can't I knuckle under to the rules set down by a handful of people who only live for power?'

Andy shook his head. 'Actually, I was thinking more along less lofty and more practical lines. Why are you helping a bunch of junior warlords get the technology to make more trouble in their part of the world – and maybe ours?'

Snowdon switched back to his suave-actor persona. He even managed to look hurt. 'The way you guys are talking, you'd think I was the bad guy in this little drama! Not so. Cetnik had an alternative program – with a fatal glitch that would leave you all dead. He really liked the propaganda possibilities – decadent American kills young people while the hard-working individuals of the Carpathian Alliance won the prize.'

He put the hand that wasn't holding the weapon on them over his heart. 'You should be thanking me! I managed to convince him not to use the killer glitch when he stopped by Milos Wallenstein's.'

David regarded the actor steadily. 'Doesn't it bother you at all to help a would-be murderer?'

That dart got through. Snowdon looked guilty for a second, but he forced his features to harden. 'Mr Cetnik was a student with a good career ahead of him when the last war started. He and the cause he supported had to live through very harsh times – caused in part by this country. If we don't like people like Slobodan Cetnik, we have to remember that we helped create him.'

'Yeah, that's what terrorists always say. "We're good

guys – you're *making* us do all these horrible things." '
Andy sneered. 'And usually we seem to cause all this
trouble simply because we're breathing.'

Snowdon's fingers went white on the grip of his hand-
pulser.

Leif decided to step in and distract him. 'Tell me
something. Wallenstein didn't have a thing to do with
Cetnik and his plan, did he? *You* were the contact who
pulled everything together at the studio.'

Snowdon looked disgusted. 'Wallenstein is a fat old
dinosaur who hasn't contributed anything new to the show
in years. I offered him scripts! I wanted to direct—'

Luckily, the actor cut that tirade off himself.

'I thought Wallenstein was committed to the anarcho-
libertarian movement,' Leif said.

'He talks about it because it's the new thing and he
wants everyone to think he's young at heart. He may even
throw money around, but does he really struggle? Is he
ready to act?'

The starfield on the forward viewscreen began to shift.
'Ah, we've taken over. Now, as long as there's no extrane-
ous input from your controls, we can bring this to an end
quickly and painlessly.'

He gave them a superior smile. 'Cetnik is also spooling a
view of this bridge specially animated to match the ship's
actions. Needless to say, I won't be appearing on it. Relax
and enjoy the ride, guys. You're out of the race. And if you
try to complain about it after the fact, well – recordings
never lie, do they?'

Snowdon was laughing at his own witticism when
another transmatter glow appeared on the already
crowded bridge. It resolved itself into a completely
unexpected figure – Ludmila Plavusa.

'Zoltan pulled us out of the ship! It's running on remote control!' she cried. 'He wouldn't explain why we shouldn't be in the simulation – but I heard him when he went outside, talking on a miniature phone with Mr Cetnik. The lethal trick – it's a defect programmed into this approach! It might kill you at any minute!'

Chapter Twenty

'That's ridiculous!' Lance Snowdon snarled, aiming the hand-pulser. '*I'm* aboard, taking care—'

'Ludmila! Cut out!' Leif yelled, hurling himself from his duty station to keep the actor from shooting her. The actor's reaction time was abysmal. Apparently, Commander Dominic's fights were fixed. Leif hit him squarely, forcing his weapons hand up over his head.

As soon as the pulser couldn't hit anybody, David shouted the emergency code that disengaged everybody from the sim.

Leif half-flung himself from his couch out there in the real world, his body continuing on in reality with the movements he'd initiated in veeyar to fight Lance Snowdon. As he righted himself, David swooped to snatch up the laptop computer. He hit one of the emergency-maneuver hot keys.

'I hope this overrides whatever they're feeding in,' he muttered. 'Otherwise they'll blow up the ship.'

'At least they won't get us with it,' Andy said, peering into the display. 'Looks like Snowdon and your blond friend bailed out too.'

David enlarged the computer's display so they could get a better look at the viewscreen. The glowing head of the comet began getting larger. 'I think this is our program!' he said.

'If we were supposed to be losing drive control, we'd be slewing around more.'

'I wonder what they're doing in C.A. Central,' Matt said, craning his neck to get a look at the Thurien ship.

The sword-ship abruptly changed course, arrowing towards the *Onrust*.

'I don't think that's remote control,' Andy said tightly.

'Zoltan must have brought his crew back in when we broke their external feed,' David said. He bit his lip.

Leif could see his friend's dilemma. Should he order them back into the *Onrust*? What if Cetnik managed to feed in the lethal order?

'Are they close enough to fire on us?' Leif asked.

Matt squinted at the screens in the display. 'Without my console readings, what you'll get is only a good guess. But no, I don't think they're quite close enough.'

Leif turned to David. 'Try the evasive-maneuvers code. That will keep us jumping around enough so they can't get us targeted.'

David nodded and input the code, accepting Leif's unspoken suggestion. *We won't go back in.*

The cometary mass danced in the forward viewscreen as the *Onrust* started corkscrewing in, jinking and zigging as if it were a fighter craft instead of a fragile racer.

We may yet tear ourselves apart with these astrobatics in the midst of all that debris, Leif though.

Red glows began showing on the image of Matt's console.

'That's bad news,' he said. 'They've probably got a fix on us.'

They hunched over the display, awaiting the laser blast that would end it all.

But it didn't come.

'Ludmila!' Leif breathed. 'I'll bet she's refusing to fire!'

The Thurien vessel finally did spit a fiery red bolt at the *Onrust*, but the human racer managed to skitter aside. The warning glow faded away.

'They lost us!' Matt shouted.

'They may not need to shoot,' David said, watching the comet's image grow. 'We're getting awfully close. One wrong zig, and we'll crash into that thing.'

'How about the Thuriens?' Leif asked. 'How close are they?'

'They've managed to overhaul us, thanks to all our jumping around,' Matt said unhappily. 'If they get a fix on us again, I don't see how they can miss.'

Leif turned to David. 'We kept the preprogrammed command for a full stop, didn't we?'

David glanced at him. 'Yes.'

'Then that's what we should do.'

'They'll blast us!' Matt and Andy protested.

'And we can't try Operation Blindfold unless we know where the Thuriens are in relation to the *Onrust*,' Leif snapped back. 'If we keep dancing around, we can't aim the sails.'

'I'll have to do it one after the other,' David muttered, more to himself than to the others.

'Just pick a good direction, and wait till they're in the right screen,' Andy suggested.

'They're dead behind us now!' Matt said urgently.

David tapped a key. The comet suddenly froze in the forward viewscreen. The sword-ship surged up in the rear-view.

He tapped another key. 'Casting our net,' he muttered.

'Contact!' Matt cried as the force-sails enveloped the Thurien vessel.

'And zap!' David stabbed down on another key.

The lights on the *Onrust*'s bridge sank even lower than they did when the special-effects crew made its announcements.

'Talk about your power drain,' Andy tried to joke.

No one paid attention. They were all staring at the rearview display. David had done well, but he was casting his net almost blindly.

For a second, the Thurien sword-ship looked like a modernistic piece of jewelry, studded here and there with diamonds and rubies. But right now, those little twinkling flashes were more valuable than any gems. They represented emitters blowing out under the hail of energy David had thrown at them.

'I don't know if we blinded 'em,' David said, looking round at his friends with a slow grin. 'But we sure poked a stick in their eyes!'

It looked as though David had called it correctly. The Thurien sword-ship dumped acceleration, almost wallowing in space. Meanwhile David was moving the *Onrust* slowly and cautiously closer to the collection of cometary fragments.

Leif's heart sank as he looked at the tiny picture representing the *Onrust*'s forward viewscreen. The comet's core was more like the old-fashioned view of an asteroid belt, with chunks of dirty ice ranging in size from boulders to young mountains tumbling about, sometimes grinding into one another, sometimes springing apart as radiation ionized off parts of their surfaces.

With only that to steer by, we're probably at least as blind as the Thuriens, Leif grimly thought. *And we don't have their options in steering the ship.*

But eyes intent and lips tight, David was evidently going to give it a try. He tapped delicately at the laptop's keyboard, initiating various simple maneuvers at very low speed. The *Onrust* crept slowly toward a large rift in the jumble of cometary matter.

From where Leif stood, it looked like an open mouth in a gargantuan face.

Like a fly zooming into a giant's mouth, he thought. *Try not to image what happens if the giant swallows.*

Matt and Andy were trying to give what aid they could, pointing out possible dangers and offering encouragement.

'You're doing fine, buddy,' Matt said tightly. 'Watch that iceberg on the left . . .'

'Past it! How's it going?' Andy asked.

Leif thought David would have glared at him in frustration if he could have taken his eyes off the screen. 'It's like . . . piloting an F-18 at full throttle – oh, no! Hah! Missed me! – using a barbell for a stick,' their captain replied in disjointed phrases.

'In short, stop jogging his elbow, you guys,' Leif warned. 'He's got enough on his mind right now.'

There was something on Leif's mind, too. He forced himself to turn away from the tense little grouping around the laptop computer and dug out his wallet. Switching it to phone function, he punched in the Net Force number on his foilpack keypad.

Captain Winters was frankly incredulous when he heard how far the Carpathian Alliance had taken its quest for a chance to pirate some new technology. But when he heard about Lance Snowdon and Slobodan Cetnik's latest ploy –

211

and how the evidence to prove what they'd been up to might be partially recorded on the Pinnacle lot – he put Leif on hold.

After waiting several minutes with muted cheers or groans coming from the peanut gallery behind him, Leif heard Winters get back on the line. 'I guess even Net Force doesn't cut much ice when these guys are filming, or whatever they call it,' Winters said. 'I finally talked to some guy named Wallenstein. He sounded pretty upset when he got the whole story and put the screws to somebody – Cosgrove?'

'Fosdyke?' Leif suggested.

'Yeah – anyway, they checked, and there's definite discrepancies between what your ship was doing and what was supposed to be happening on the bridge. I've got our L.A. office trying to trace the tap this C.A. agent is using. If we can catch him with the goods—'

Behind Leif, three voices rose in almost savage exultation.

'What's going on there?'

Leif whipped round to peer at the computer screen in disbelief.

'Against all odds, David just managed to tag the finish buoy,' he replied. 'If he can keep us alive for a few more minutes, we'll win the race.'

David did not have an easy time jockeying them out of the comet's nucleus using the laptop's keyboard rather than the sensitive controls he could've accessed from veeyar. On top of that, the racket of a landing helicopter tore through the flimsily constructed Casa Falldown during some of the most difficult maneuvers.

'What the heck is that?' Matt craned his neck, trying to look out the streaked window.

'What I want to know is how anybody could write in here?' Andy growled, his attention split between the screen and a growing altercation down the hall.

Through the gap in the doorway, Leif saw a protesting Slobodan Cetnik being escorted through the hall by FBI Net Force officers.

One of the agents carried a laptop computer that looked like a twin to David's.

As the Net Force Explorers went down to breakfast the next morning, they discovered a surprise guest in the lobby – Captain Winters.

'Congratulations on winning that race,' the captain told them. 'Although I hear Pinnacle Studios is now doing some very fast footwork.' He sighed. 'To be frank, so is the State Department.'

'Politics.' Leif pronounced it as though it were a dirty word.

'They both have a vested interest in keeping this whole story covered up.'

'Oh, yeah,' Andy said bitterly. 'Don't upset the Carpathian Alliance. Yes, they're openly hostile to us, and we caught them dabbling in what looks suspiciously like cyber-terrorism, but it's not diplomatic to *offend* them.'

Matt, however, got right to the point. 'What brings you out here, Captain Winters?'

'Somehow, I don't think it's just to congratulate us,' Leif said.

Winters gave him a half-grin. 'It's partly your fault, Anderson. I have a very brief field mission, liaising with our office here in L.A. After all, I was the guy who put them on to this whole Carpathian mess, after you called me.'

'So how do you expect this all to shake out?' Leif asked.

The captain shrugged. 'I expect Pinnacle Studios will stand by the results of the race, although when the episode comes out, you can expect the end will be heavily edited for holovision. That actor guy – Snowdon – after finally realizing that Cetnik would have happily killed him to pull off his little stunt, he got furious. In spite of the efforts of a flock of Pinnacle lawyers, he's been talking his head off to the FBI. They're building an entire file about how the Carpathian Alliance has penetrated anarcho-libertarian splinter factions.'

'That isn't going to help the movement's political chances,' Leif said.

Winters shrugged. 'Again, it all depends on how much gets out.' He looked almost embarrassed as he spoke next. 'A former high-ranking member of the FBI heads their technical division. He's been a Frontie all his life.'

'So Commander Dominic may just swashbuckle his way through this one,' David said. 'How about Mr Cetnik?'

'If State sits on what he did here, the guy may walk,' Winters admitted. 'I'm going to have a little personal chat with him, though. Point out to him that, considering his failure, there may be some things he wouldn't like his home government to know.' He glanced at Leif. 'It's the least we can do for that girl who helped you.'

Speaking of which . . .

'Thanks for telling me. I'll try and pass that along to her. But Captain . . . guys . . . you'll have to excuse me now. I have an appointment.'

Rising from his seat, Leif picked up the plainly wrapped package he'd retrieved from the front desk. It had been delivered by messenger from his father's L.A. offices.

Leif tucked it under his arm and headed out to the hotel's courtyard and pool.

Ludmila Plavusa perched on the edge of one of the deck chairs, squinting at the people happily splashing in the pool. Although she wore a bathing suit and sat out in the sun, she acted as though she were chilled.

'I thought you'd need these,' Leif said, reaching into his shirt pocket. He pulled out the sunglasses he'd bought for her during their all-too-brief outing.

She responded with a wan smile as she put them on. 'My only souvenir of this visit to sunny California.' Then she rubbed her arms. 'I'm afraid it may be a long, cold winter.'

If this were a holo-drama, Leif thought, *I'd tell her I loved her and that I'd arranged for political asylum. She'd leap into my arms, happily forgetting about her family and her homeland.*

But this was real life, and he had to get real. 'It may not be that bad,' he said quietly. 'My connection to Net Force has arrived to put a few well-chosen words in Cetnik's ear. He may not be so eager to tell the whole story of his fiasco when he gets back to the C.A.'

Ludmila seemed a little taken aback. 'They'd do that for me?'

'You helped us,' Leif pointed out. 'Your warning saved our lives – and may have helped crack this case open. If you ask me, it's the least we could do.'

'Ah,' she said, looking up at his eyes. 'For the case. Of course.'

Leif felt a warmth on his cheeks that didn't come from the sun. 'That's not even counting my personal feelings.'

'Personal?' For just a second, a little laughing devil looked out of her big blue eyes.

Leif gave her a look. 'Oh, stop trying to twist my tail and scoot over on that stupid chair.'

Silently, she did as he asked. Leif sat beside her.

'We've only known one another a few days, but they've certainly been jam-packed,' he said. 'When I finally got to know you – well, you weren't what I expected.'

'You either,' she admitted.

'Anyway, I thought you should have something more than a pair of sunglasses to remember our time together. So I managed to get you this.'

He passed over the package. Ludmila removed the plain wrappings and began to laugh. It was the laptop computer Leif's father had attempted to market.

'I'm afraid they never really sold,' Leif said. 'The technology seems too dated. There's a warehouse full of them out here.' He cleared his throat. 'I also got a replacement for Alex de Courcy. But I thought you'd like to own one, free and clear.' He wagged a warning finger. 'Just don't let your government grab it.'

She flung an arm around his shoulders. 'What a smooth talker,' she said with a laugh, 'giving me an old piece of junk.'

Her blue eyes were on a level with his. For a second, the laughter faded. They both considered possibilities . . . might-have-beens.

'We'll always have Hollywood,' Ludmila said quietly. She kissed him on each cheek, European style.

Then she kissed him on the lips.

David caught up with Leif sometime later. 'You know, you're going to get burned.'

I will, if the Customs people ever find out about that computer, Leif thought. He looked up quickly. 'Huh?'

'I said, you're going to get burned if you keep sitting outside in this sun,' David looked at his friend. 'She said good-bye?'

'We both said good-bye,' Leif replied. 'At least there'll be some good memories attached to all this.'

'We *did* win,' David pointed out. 'Matt and Andy are still inside, arguing over who should get what.'

'Count me out. Your guys earned whatever you can get. Besides, I've got enough new toys in my apartment to keep me busy,' Leif said.

David shook his head, smiling wryly. 'You really want nothing?'

'Hey, I'll have my memories. And a datascrip of the Great Race episode, once it's ready.' Leif smiled back. 'We should be glad to get out of here with our lives.'

David laughed. 'Amen to that,' he said. 'This place makes great fantasies—'

Leif finished. 'But the real life out here is too weird to believe.'